Drumbeat

T0352600

Drumbeat

Mohamed El-Bisatie

Translated by
Peter Daniel

The American University in Cairo Press
Cairo   New York

This paperback edition published in 2015 by
The American University in Cairo Press
113 Sharia Kasr el Aini, Cairo, Egypt
420 Fifth Avenue, New York, NY 10018
www.aucpress.com

Exclusive distribution outside Egypt and North America by I.B. Tauris & Co Ltd.,
6 Salem Road, London, W4 2BU

Dar el Kutub No. 7551/15
ISBN 978 977 416 733 1

Dar el Kutub Cataloging-in-Publication Data

El-Bisatie, Mohamed
        Drumbeat / Mohamed El-Bisatie.—Cairo: The American University
    in Cairo Press, 2015.
        p.   cm.
        ISBN 978 977 416 733 1
        1. English fiction
        823

1 2 3 4 5   19 18 17 16 15

Designed by Fatiha Bouzidi
Printed in Egypt

1

came to the Emirate to work, like thousands of others from various parts of the world. The discovery of oil here many years ago had changed everything overnight. Modern skyscrapers shot up, sheathed in smoked-glass façades to repel the scorching sun. Huge multistoried malls proliferated with their banks of gleaming escalators. So did amusement parks featuring the most state-of-the-art rides. Water mains and drainage systems were installed, roads were dug and paved, bridges and flyovers climbed to two and three levels, and row after row of trees and shrubbery were laid out, even along the narrowest streets, and this greenery now stretches to the edge of the desert where it thins out into rings encircling the huge greenhouses that have been erected here and there for cultivating fruits and vegetables. As construction boomed and the city sprawled, suburbs were born: complexes of grand and ornately embellished villas, each with its own swimming pool and set in spacious gardens, every tree, bush, and flower of which had been nurtured from seedlings flown in from abroad.

We foreign workers are a hodgepodge of different nationalities. Most are from the Philippines, probably because of their reputation for being fast and serious workers. Perhaps, too, because they are small and compact and so do not take up much room. Somehow this makes their Emirati employers feel more comfortable when dealing with them.

The Indians crammed themselves into one part of the old town. They took over the entire quarter. The other nationalities respected their communal urge and so did not try to move in on them. The Pakistanis took over an adjacent quarter, while the Arabs and other foreigners dispersed themselves over other parts of the city. Despite their historic animosity, the Indians and Pakistanis socialize together frequently and visit the same nightspots in each other's quarters. But, every time tensions mount between India and Pakistan and their respective armies amass along their borders, an invisible barrier shoots up between the two quarters, the exchange of family visits ceases, and not so much as a "hello" passes between the two sides.

The old town is separated from the modern part of the Emirati capital by vast tracts of scrub brush. The houses in these quarters huddle closely together. One or two stories high, their walls are made of mud and their roofs of wood. Yet these simple structures have weathered countless years since they first served to gather in the indigenous inhabitants from their far-flung tents in the desert.

With modernization came renovations. Clean water was piped in; bathrooms were fitted with the latest toilets, tubs, sinks, automatic washing machines, and water heaters; floors were encased with ceramic tiles and parquet; and air conditioners and fans were mounted on the walls and ceilings. In addition, the old quarters were given a new sewer system to take the place of the open ditches that once cleaved their way through the streets and alleys, carrying reeking human excrement into the desert where it poured into neat rows of deep pits that were backfilled once they were full. In the old days, the people would cover the sewer ditches with whatever sheets of tin, planks of wood, or scraps of burlap bags they could get hold of. But the stench still pursued them wherever they went, only lessening slightly when they went into their homes and shut all the doors and windows.

They say that after oil was discovered and the building boom began, there was a debate over whether to raze the old town. The major objection was that many people would want to pay the occasional visit to their ancestral homes and the pastures of their youth. Ultimately, it was decided to let the old quarters stand, renovate them in a manner that preserved their historic character and then reconsider tearing them down after a generation or two. Therefore, you can still see some antique lamps hanging on the street corners, crowns of palm trees peering out from above interior courtyards, and the sloping pigeon cotes on the rooftops with those little round windows high up on their walls, no bigger than peepholes.

Foreign workers generally settled in the old town because the rents were cheap. Also, conditions were such that they could live at ease amid their familiar din.

2

like to spend my free evenings in the old town. The coffeehouses stay open until all hours. Portable glass-encased
grills are rolled out to the street corners, and tables and
chairs are arranged around them. Music, laughter, and the
fragrances of every imaginable type of food fill the air.

Emiratis sometimes bring their foreign guests here. They
arrive in their huge SUVs and after touring the neighborhood
they leave their cars, weave their way through the sidewalk
cafés, and settle down for a bite to eat at one of the food
stands. Occasionally, the owners of these stands are overcome
by a spirit of gallantry and try to refuse payment. Generally,
these are newcomers from Syria or Egypt. They dry their
hands on the towels hanging over their shoulders and say to
the Emirati host, "Your guests are my guests. The honor of
your coming is payment enough." The Emirati responds with
a glare, places some cash on the table, and leaves.

Some foreign workers are live-in servants in Emirati palaces
and villas. That is the case with me. I have a slightly senior position, being the personal driver of the owner of the villa where
I work, though he often prefers to drive himself. A wealthy

sheikh of about forty, we servants call him Abu Amer—the father of Amer—as do his friends. He owns four warehouses out of which he sells imported automobile parts and electrical appliances wholesale. After meeting the demands of the domestic market, he sells the surplus to various countries that suffered hard currency shortages. His way around this problem is to accept payment in kind, on the condition that he chooses the products himself: ready-made cotton clothes, embroidered textiles, antique pieces of inlaid furniture, and other handicrafts that breathe the spirit of their country of origin. These he re-exports to his large retail stores in Paris, Berlin, and New York. I saw for myself, in one of his outlets in Paris, Egyptian clothes and textiles, tapestries woven in the village of Kardasa in Giza, several articles of furniture that were billed in the window display as manufactured in Damietta, and a large array of silverwork: decorative platters and bowls, and necklaces, earrings, and bracelets. All these items were tagged with prices at least ten times higher than what they cost in Egypt. One day, to my surprise, I noticed a large display of those small palm-frond crates used by Egyptian vegetable vendors. They were all the rage. Parisian housewives flocked into the store to buy them and left with as many as they could carry. A single crate was going for ten francs. In my village, at the time, they cost the equivalent of a quarter of a franc.

I often see Abu Amer walking in the garden of his palace, mobile glued to his ear, barking out orders in English, which I speak well, this being one of the required qualifications for my employment. When it comes to work, he generally makes his phone calls away from his family who complain whenever his mind strays in the middle of a conversation and he snatches up his mobile to call someone on a work-related matter.

There are five Pakistani maids to clean the villa and to cook. They sleep in an annex with three bedrooms and a living room. I live in the annex on the opposite side of the villa, next to the garage, with three Filipinos. We each have our own bedroom. Two of them are in charge of maintaining the grounds, trimming the shrubbery, cleaning the swimming pool, and a variety of odd jobs. I see them in the morning at breakfast and again in the evening before they go to bed. The third is in charge of the cars belonging to Abu Amer's wife and two daughters, both of whom are of marriageable age. The women prefer to drive their own cars, but he has to be on hand in case one of them asks him to chauffeur. He also has to drive little Amer to school or wherever and return later to pick him up and bring him back.

The Filipinos are not easy to communicate with. When speaking with others they use a mixture of English and Arabic, and if they cannot find the words they need, they resort to mimes and gestures. It amuses me to observe all their frowns, ums and ahs, and comical facial contortions when they are stuck for a way to convey what they want to say.

I look after both of Abu Amer's cars—one's a Land Rover, the other a sedan—and take the wheel when he tells me to. Even if he drives, I still have to accompany him. So decreed his wife, Umm Amer, after he lost his way several times in the streets of the Emirate and began to pile up driving fines.

He has me sit beside him in the passenger seat. He has the habit of thinking out loud while driving, about shipments that are past their deadline, for example, and how much that will cost him: "The late penalty? Sure I'll take the late penalty. But what good does it do? Once you're stuck with delivery dates? The customers keep nagging you day in, day out. And

6

you keep having to think up excuses to put them off. What a pain, huh? Isn't it a pain?"

He shoots me a sideways glance. I keep my eyes on the road ahead and my mouth shut. It's plain enough that he's being friendly and anticipates a comment, but I'm cautious. Even when he says something meant to make me laugh, I keep my face blank, until he nudges me with his elbow, at which point I smile faintly.

He sighs and falls silent. Then he starts thinking aloud again. His wife and daughters want to go clothes shopping in Rome. This could not come at a more inconvenient time. If they could only wait a couple of weeks, then maybe he could go with them, but . . . .

In addition to accompanying him around the Emirate, I sometimes escort him on his trips abroad, particularly to Paris. There my job is to act as his bodyguard.

Paris is strictly for R & R. He never does business there; doesn't even talk about work. He has an apartment on the Champs-Elysées, where he regularly spends a couple of weeks a year, not counting spur-of-the-moment trips. He hires a car with a driver by the day. Still, he counts on my services. He goes out to the nightclubs—discotheques, strip joints, and the like. He'd heard of too many incidents of people getting mugged around those places. He told me stories of Arabs, mostly, who had had their money and passports stolen. When we go out, he gives me his passport and a wad of cash for emergencies. I also carry a jackknife. I've only had to use it once. Abu Amer was coming out of a nightclub, walking slightly unsteadily, even though he doesn't drink. Maybe he was still dazed by the erotic spectacle inside. He craned his neck to find our hired car. When he spotted it he started to walk over. The chauffeur remained behind the wheel, but I had gotten out when I saw Abu Amer and was leaning with my back against the car. Suddenly, three men appeared out of nowhere and headed straight toward Abu Amer. He froze and his eyes darted around in alarm. Something drew my attention to the hand of one of the attackers: the flash of brass knuckles. I reached Abu Amer before they did, placed myself in front of him and flicked open my jackknife. The hand with the brass knuckles flew at my face. I lashed out with the knife. The man yelped, fell back, and scuttled off. The two others circled around us. A foot came toward my groin. The blade slashed the leg attached to it. The man attached to that groaned and doubled over in pain. The third man remained standing as Abu Amer and I backed our way to the car. The driver by now had gotten out and was leaning against the car. He asked us, in English, whether we were all right.

"We're okay," Abu Amer responded angrily. "But at least you could have sounded the horn."

"I couldn't," the driver answered as he slid back into his seat. "They would have been on the lookout for me if I had and they probably would have told others. You could have just given them twenty francs. All they wanted was enough for a bit to drink. And a bit to snort."

"Then you know who they are."

"I know no one."

Abu Amer is a completely different person in Paris. He becomes smooth and dapper: off goes the long, white thawb and on comes the tailored suit, a flashy tie, and a matching handkerchief in the breast pocket of his jacket. He exudes a heavy perfume, and his hair—newly coiffed in a fashionable style—shines slightly.

In the morning, he takes up a station in a sidewalk café, intently watching the people coming and going while he has breakfast. He has me sit with him until his friends come, after which I move to a nearby table.

There was this girlfriend, once, who had come to live in the apartment. Twenty years old, in a miniskirt and skimpy blouse held up by two thin straps and revealing the sides of her breasts. I'd never stay in the apartment for more than a few minutes, just long enough to put away the shopping in the kitchen. Then I'd return to my room in the small hotel in which I was quartered and wait there.

I rarely saw her. But once it was she who answered the door. Her face was very pale and dark circles rimmed her eyes. With one hand, she held her straggly hair out of her face. She had almost nothing on. She stared at me blankly for a while and then finally recognized me. She let go of the door and disappeared into her room.

The last time I saw her was after she had been with Abu Amer for about three years. She had grown even paler and her cheeks had acquired a yellow tinge. She let me in without saying a word, then went into the living room and stood looking out of the closed window. She was wearing one of Abu Amer's shirts, its tails tied around her belly. Her panties were on crooked. One side was twisted under the waistband, leaving a buttock exposed. She seemed oblivious. I took the bags I was carrying into the kitchen, unpacked their contents into the cupboards and the fridge, and left.

Another took her place. She looked very much like her predecessor had three years earlier—the same boyish figure, thick chestnut hair, bright smile and light step, like a bird hopping on the verge of taking flight. Like her predecessor, too, she would throw her arms around his neck and cling to him tightly as she spoke to him, undeterred by his grumbled protests and attempts to wriggle free.

3

ime passes quietly in the Emirate. Evenings are spent watching television or in family visits, or at the occasional dinner party or birthday celebration. In the summer, many Emirati families leave for European shores. Therefore, when the national soccer team qualified for the World Cup the effect was akin to an explosion. Emiratis, together with the foreign workers, thronged the streets, shouting wildly and waving the national flag and photos of the soccer players. Microphones blared, horns honked, and cheerers were hoisted onto others' shoulders in impromptu parades. The team had been trying to qualify for years, changing coaches several times. With the latest coach—the one from Spain—they made the breakthrough. After a series of victories against visiting teams, they scored several more against other countries in their division, bringing them to the World Cup playoffs.

The Emirate was swept up into many days of ecstatic jubilation. His Royal Highness the Emir issued an edict ordering government agencies to disburse an extra month's salary as a bonus to all government employees, and he urged non-government businesses and organizations to do likewise. But even without the bonus we would have rejoiced at the achievement of the national team.

The World Cup games that year were going to be held in France. My Filipino colleagues and I began to set up a corner of the garage for the occasion. We bought several poufs to sit on and built up stores of cold drinks, light snacks, and charcoal and tobacco. During their visits to their friends in the old quarters, the Filipinos had learned how to smoke the narghile from the resident Arab workers. Evidently, word of our preparations had reached Abu Amer, because he appeared in the garage one morning to have a look. He smiled and left. Before long, he sent down a large wide-screen television to take the place of our small set, as well as several more cushions and a couple of small coffee tables.

Huge electronic display screens were erected in the main squares, public gardens, and bus stations. Alongside them were billboards showing the national soccer team gathered around their coach. The photo was captioned with the Quranic verse, *If God aids you, none can conquer you.*

As the playoffs approached and enthusiasm mounted, His Royal Highness proclaimed that Emirati citizens should travel to France to support the team and that the government would foot all travel and accommodation costs. He further decreed that all citizens currently residing abroad should head to France to receive the team. This was a national duty of the first order, the emir stated.

In the capitol building, ledgers were drawn up listing all Emirati citizens, the names of the hotels and the room numbers that had been reserved for them in France, and their time of departure. How many were they? More than thirty thousand? Over a period of six days, swarms of airplanes took off, returned, and took off again. Abu Amer and his family left on the sixth day. I stood by the Land Rover at the foot of the front stairs of the villa, waiting for them to come out. Abu Amer issued no parting instructions. There was no need to. Each member of his domestic staff knows his or her job very well. Often he calls me into the house when he is unable to find the television channel he is looking for. He subscribes to three satellite networks and although I have explained to him how it works innumerable times he keeps forgetting how to tune into them. He also leaves the affairs of his stores and warehouses to their managers, only intervening when an urgent matter has to be brought to his attention. I was with him once when he was called in to deal with an emergency that cropped up in one of his warehouses. I was waiting by the door until Abu Amer finished business inside the manager's office. After the manager—a Syrian who had served the company for many years—related the problem, Abu Amer issued instructions. They were completely opposite to what the manager had expected. The customer, a wealthy Emirati, stood up, a satisfied smile on his face. The Syrian manager hesitated a moment, shifting his eyes back and forth between Abu Amer and the customer. Then he addressed Abu Amer, "If your decision is motivated by personal reasons, that's something else. I'll record this in the documents so that it doesn't apply to the other contracts."

"What do you mean?" asked Abu Amer.

"I mean that your decision runs counter to the provisions of the contract you signed with this gentleman."

"How so?"

"There was no provision in the contract stipulating that changes in the exchange rates would apply. Therefore, the price originally stated in the contract is binding on both parties. If the rates had changed in the opposite direction, we would have had to sustain the loss."

Abu Amer looked down for a moment, and then said, "Do as you see fit. You know better." Then he turned to the customer and smiled, "As you see, it's out of my hands."

"Out of your hands? That's going to cost me," protested the customer.

"Well, then it's going to cost you. What's right is right," responded Abu Amer as he hooked his arm around the customer's and escorted him out of the office.

4

waited at the airport until the last flock of airplanes took off. Abu Amer and his family had left for France. I drove back to town.

The highway was deserted. As I approached the outskirts of the city a thought occurred to me that made me laugh. The whole country was now in the hands of the foreign workers. If they took over the Emirate, closed the ports, and broadcast an impassioned message to the world demanding recognition for their new regime, on the grounds that everything in the country was built with their toil and sweat, they could well receive some international recognition. I recalled a somewhat similar scenario in one of the neighboring emirates. Apparently, the fifty-year-old crown prince there felt that he had waited long enough for his turn to rule. All that stood between him and the throne was his elderly father's relatively robust health. The emir still took his daily morning exercise of long jaunts on his white steed. More infuriating yet were those occasional evening gatherings that the emir hosted in the palace garden for his children and close friends. At the height of the festivities, a couple of servants would appear bearing a thick wooden cane that they would set atop two sturdy wooden supports planted in the ground. The king would then step forward as he rolled up his sleeve, lift his arm up and thrust the edge of his palm downward, karate-style, chopping the cane in two. The display elicited appreciative applause and exclamations from all, apart from the crown prince who would erupt in a coughing fit to disguise his fury.

Then came that day when the old man left for medical treatment abroad. It was only for a few tests to reassure himself. He had no serious complaints. The crown prince, together with other senior officials, saw him off at the airport. He kissed his father on both cheeks as the father patted his son's hefty shoulder. Exactly two days later, while his father was settled in his private wing in the hospital, the crown prince seized power and was proclaimed the new emir. When the news reached the elderly sheikh, he leaped from his hospital bed shouting, "I have to leave now!" He bolted down the corridors wearing only his short white hospital gown and dragging the IV stand behind him as the nurses rushed after him to detach the needles from his arms. He was intercepted by several of his private guards, who were staying with him in the hospital. He glowered at them and said, "And what about you?" They looked down nervously and shuffled their feet, unable to understand his question. He turned and headed back to the ward. "Check me out of here and get me back to the hotel. We're going home tonight."

Later that day the old emir held a press conference that was aired on all the radio and television stations. He was returning to the Emirate to discipline his wayward son. He would personally slap his face in front of everyone, he vowed.

16

His son quickly broadcast a response: "Don't come back, father. I beg you not to come back. I will not step down. You will always remain my father whom I will cherish and revere. But please, do not return."

I had the opportunity to watch this speech. His chubby face quivered and a tear formed in his right eye and glistened in the light of the cameras. Just as it was on the verge of falling, he wiped it away with a finger.

The deposed emir appealed to several friendly governments to help restore him to power. Eventually his wrath subsided, perhaps because these friendly governments were not especially keen to help although they were more than happy to welcome him as their guest.

5

Nothing changed. Life in the city continued as normal.
People tended to their usual business. Shoppers went
into stores and came out laden with bags. Pakistani
and Indian women still rolled baby carriages toward public
parks. The only differences were that the street-sweeping
vehicles appeared earlier than usual and that the amusement
park lights came on well before nightfall. I've always wanted
to ride on one of those Ferris wheels and feel the thrill of
swooping back and forth in one of those tiny boxes high up in
the air amid the multilingual babble of shouts and screams.

I pulled into the estate and brought the Land Rover to
a stop in front of the garage. I got out and looked for the
Filipino groundkeepers. They were nowhere to be found. I
spotted the Pakistani women at the entrance to the garden
trying to suppress their smiles. I asked them, in English,
where my colleagues were. They pointed toward the pool
house at the far end of the garden and giggled as they fled
into their quarters.

The aqua-colored swimming pool is surrounded on all
sides by deck chairs and tables. On one side a door leads to

the bathrooms and changing rooms. Behind a second door a stairway leads to the interior of the villa.

The Filipinos were in their swimming suits, frolicking loudly in the pool, splashing water in all directions. They beckoned me to join them. I laughed. Their clothes were strewn over the chairs. On one of the tables stood a large tray filled with thermoses of hot drinks, cups, and a plate of cookies. I made myself a cup of tea, sat down, and waited until they finished.

After we came out of the pool house, one of the Pakistani women approached us and asked, "Why don't you have dinner with us in the garden?"

The other women came over and stood alongside her, looking at me with gentle smiles. Apparently the Filipinos were in on this. They must have assumed that as an Arab I stood as the head of the household in the absence of its masters. The moment this occurred to me, I felt that I had to dispel that impression from the outset. I said, "I'm just one of you. Each of us should feel free to do as he or she likes. But if one of us wants to leave the grounds, say to spend the night somewhere else, we should leave the address. That way if that person is away longer than expected, the rest of us will know where to start looking."

From the subsequent exchange of looks and gestures I gathered that they agreed. The Pakistani woman asked me how long the Emiratis were going to be away. I replied, "About a month. We'll know by watching the playoffs."

We all took part in the preparations for our banquet in the middle of the garden. We covered the dining table with a long embroidered tablecloth with fringed edges and set it with the finest china and crystal in the house. Eventually, two large platters were placed in the center, each with a large fish on it, one grilled and the other fried. Ice-cold cans of soft drinks were within reach on an adjacent serving table.

The men sat on one side, the women on the other. Contrary to custom their heads were uncovered and their long hair fell in thick braids down their backs.

One of them boasted, "No one knows fish like I do. I went to the market by myself and picked them out. I'm the one who cooked them, too."

"I made the rice. And I helped you fry the fish," said another.

"No you didn't."

"Yes I did. I poured the oil into the frying pan."

The women laughed.

The food was delicious. I hadn't tasted anything like it since I'd been in the Emirate. Afterward we stretched out on deck chairs among the flowering shrubbery, sipped our cold drinks, and chatted about this and that in our blend of broken English and gestures. We then put water to boil in the electric kettle we had brought out, made ourselves tea, fresh coffee, or Nescafé and returned to our seats where we sat silently, contemplating our surroundings as though we had never seen them before.

One of the Filipinos sighed and said, "Life is beautiful." The "beautiful" he accentuated by kissing the tips of his fingers and flicking them outward in the air.

"That's stupid," commented one of his colleagues.

"Like you say," responded the first.

That was the real icebreaker. We spoke about our families in our faraway homes and about the days of our youth. One of the Pakistanis said that she was supporting a whole alleyway in her hometown. Seven families lived there, all related.

We agreed that one of the women should take charge of our expenses while our boss and his family were away. The villa was well stocked, but we decided that we would split the expenses for any extra food or drink that we bought. The woman who supported an entire alley said that Umm Amer had left some money with her for household expenses. After that ran out, we would start paying out of our own pockets.

"What are we going to do tonight?" asked one of the Filipinos. "And don't say 'watch television.' We do that every night. Think of something fun, something that will make me die laughing."

"How about the amusement park? I still haven't been there," said another.

His two compatriots were enthusiastic. The first turned to the rest of us and asked, "How about you? Do you want to come too?" Meeting my silence—I was simply turning the idea around in my head—he said, "Anyway, afterward we'll be going on to visit some people we know in the old town."

We drank another round of coffee.

The shadows cast by the setting sun had inched their way across the lawn and begun to crawl up the tree trunks. The next time I looked they had reached the branches.

One of the Pakistanis leaned forward and said that she wanted to tell us something, but swore us to secrecy. After a moment's pause, during which she exchanged glances with the other women, she said, "One of us is married—Rishim." She indicated one of her four companions who lowered her eyes and smiled shyly. The first woman continued, "She lied about her marriage because one of Umm Amer's conditions was that we had to be single. At first it was easy to keep her marriage a secret because her husband was in Pakistan. But nine months ago he got a contract to work in the Emirate. He works in road construction and now he's living in the old town. He shares a room with two others. They haven't dared to meet. If Umm Amer found out, she'd fire her. All they can do is write to each other once in a while. Several months ago he wrote to ask her to meet him in the supermarket near here. He had found out where we lived. He'd even passed by our house several times, but had never dared to stop and look. Rishim went to the supermarket on the pretext that she had to buy some milk and envelopes. She saw him there, but she didn't try to speak with him. She was afraid that one of the other customers in the supermarket might know Umm Amer and tell her that she saw one of her maids talking to a foreigner. That's something Umm Amer would never allow. She's warned us many times against speaking with strangers. She's afraid that one of them will sneak into the villa while everyone's asleep. I have no idea how that idea ever occurred to her."

She fell silent and looked down. All the others did as well, except for Rishim who stared absently toward the bushes, a faint smile playing on her face. The first resumed, "They caught him once. He knows which part of the villa she lives in. She should never have given him that information. It was a big mistake. He let her know the day and time that he planned on passing by. She stood on a chair in one of our rooms that overlooks the street in the back and watched him walking back and forth. She could see him, but he couldn't see her. So the next time he wrote to her he asked her to wave at him, just so he'd know where her room was. We warned her not to and she took our advice. But all that walking back and forth drew attention. One day the police came and took him into the station. The sergeant in charge there is an Indian. That's how it is, as you know. They're all Indians there because of a security agreement with India. Each station has a man from Pakistan, another from the Philippines, and a third from some other Arab country. But those are hired for janitorial work and other services. Only the Indians can give orders, after the police chief who's an Emirati. Anyway, the Indian sergeant in the station knows Rishim's husband. He goes to the old town sometimes to spend a night out or visit relatives. He'd seen Rishim's husband in a coffeehouse there and remembered him. The Indian sergeant leaned toward him and told him to tell the chief that he'd been looking for his friend, the sergeant, but kept getting lost and didn't know how to ask directions in any language but his own. When Rishim's husband said this, the chief burst out laughing and said, 'A Pakistani looking for an Indian . . . . It must be love!'

"The chief didn't believe the story. He had her husband sent to the police station in the old town with instructions to make the necessary inquiries and act accordingly. There he was released but the Indian sergeant warned him to stay in the old town and to take care because he was under temporary surveillance. He hasn't showed up here since and he's stopped writing too. A Pakistani friend of ours was visiting some relatives of hers in the old town and we asked her to find out what she could. She learned that he's well and that he's planning on returning to his village in a month for a two-week holiday. Rishim can't go. Umm Amer won't give us leave.

"When I asked for a holiday last month she said, 'Why would you want to go to your country? Everything you could possibly want is right here.'

"'I'd like to see my family, Umm Amer.'

23

"'We're like family to you. These days I need every single one of you. Be patient. As you can see there's so much to do. There's so much work that it keeps all of you busy from morning to night. I think I might even have to hire two more maids . . . . Have your family send you letters. Pictures. Cassette tapes so you can hear their voices. Be patient. Then in two or three months, God willing . . . .'

"I know Umm Amer. When she gets used to things being a certain way she hates any change."

As I listened, I kept wondering why this woman was telling us all this. I expected the answer soon. The Filipino sitting next to me had had some difficulty following her story and would occasionally ask her to repeat whole segments. Eventually, however, she sat back in her chair and we turned to Rishim. The young woman felt uncomfortable with all our eyes on her. She bowed her head and fidgeted with her braid. But the smile never left her face.

The woman who had told us Rishim's story turned to the Filipino who had made the suggestion of going to the amusement park and asked, "Are you really going to the old town after the amusement park?"

"That's the plan."

"If we gave you his address, would you take a letter to him and bring back an answer if you find him?"

The Filipino next to me was Umm Amer's driver. He leaned forward excitedly. "What do you mean, 'take a letter and bring back an answer?' I'll go there myself and fetch him."

"Who?"

"Her husband. Didn't you say he was her husband? Give me the address."

"You mean you're going to bring him here? To the villa?"

24

"Sure, why not?"

She studied our faces for a moment then said, "I don't know. We have to think."

"What's there to think about? It's a simple matter. He's her husband and he should see her. Give me the address."

All eyes turned to me waiting for my go-ahead. "I'm just one of you," I reminded them.

"I'll take the car and get him," the driver said. "He can stay here until they get back from France."

"Where's he going to sleep?" asked the woman who spoke for Rishim.

"In Amer's room."

"That's the best place," put in a second Filipino.

The women exchanged glances then huddled into a whispered consultation, except for Rishim, who stood to the side, eyes averted. It did not take long for them to reach an agreement. After they gave the driver the address, one of them took Rishim's hand and led her inside. The others followed.

The driver, now holding the address in his hand, headed toward the car. One of his mates rushed after him and said, "Take me with you."

"Don't park near his house," I called out after them.

"Why?" one of them asked. "No one will know why we're there."

I watched them get into the car and drive out of the grounds.

6

The remaining Filipino and I pulled up a couple of seats in front of the garage. The footpaths leading through the grounds to the villa were bathed in the soft light of dozens of little shin-high lamps. A fragrant incense had begun to curl through the air. We sat for a while contemplating my colleague's delicate smoke rings as they wafted upward and vanished. The women's songs and giggles floated out from inside the villa. Then there was silence. They were getting her ready.

Finally, they emerged. Rishim led the procession, like a bride. Her face glistened in the footpath lights. She wore a long dress and an embroidered shawl. Her hair had been drawn up to form a crown which was interlaced with tiny white flowers. They ascended the two stairs to the door and paused on the landing, where they chanted what seemed like a prayer. Rishim went inside. The other four remained for a moment on the doorstep, then turned and returned to their quarters.

The car pulled into the driveway and pulled to a stop before the front door. One of the Filipinos escorted the Pakistani who seemed to stagger slightly as he walked. He had some garment flung over his shoulder—a jacket or a jallabiya; it

26

was difficult to tell. He stooped to remove his sandals, but the Filipino indicated to him to keep them on. The Filipino reappeared several minutes later with a wide grin on his face. He pointed to me and said, "In Arabic you say 'tamam.' In English, 'okay!'" He gave a loud laugh. "Now, to the amusement park. You coming?"

"Maybe I'll catch you later." I gestured toward the villa. "What about him?"

"He's um . . . ."

"I mean his job. Doesn't he have to work in the morning?"

"Oh that!" He laughed again. "They're taking the day off tomorrow. All of them. They called up their boss in France and he agreed because he's so happy about the team. You should see them in the old town. They've taken all the tables and chairs out of the coffeehouses and set them up in the streets and on the sidewalks. They're singing and yelling and dancing. A man from your country is doing some kind of cane dance to the music of bamboo flutes and drums."

"And the day after tomorrow?"

"He can take the bus to the place where his company's buses pick them up and take them to work. After work, he'll come back here. He's arranged everything. Come on, why don't you come with us?"

"I have something to do first. I'll catch up with you later. Ask the girls. Maybe they'd like to go."

"Hey, that's right." He called them up on his mobile. After he hung up, he said, "They're going to stay here. They're making some food for the 'wedding couple.' Anyway they don't want to leave them all alone here."

The Filipinos piled into the car and left.

7

I cast a quick look back at the garage and then left, too — on foot. I walked around the perimeter of the villa, not because I was afraid of thieves, but just as a routine precaution. Once, it paid off: I discovered sparks sputtering from bare wires jutting out from a tear in some exposed electricity tubing in the wall. I had never heard of a single incident of theft since I had been in the Emirate. I have heard of swindling and fraud, but not burglary. To each country its own thieves. What is there to steal from the villas and palaces anyway? The owners keep all their money in the banks, and jewelry and other valuables are stashed in heavy-duty safes. Electrical appliances? It would hardly be worth the risk; they're so cheap here.

As I walked I mulled over the unexpected turn in the situation inside the villa. It bothered me slightly. If Abu Amer found out I would be in a tougher spot than the rest of them; of all the domestic staff I was the closest to him. What if he asked me, "And you? Did you go along with them?" I could picture the look on his face if I replied that I had.

Suddenly, there was a rapid succession of booms and colorful arcs began to fill the night sky. Fireworks. Everyone must be out celebrating.

I jerked my head toward the sound of a whisper from the next door villa. A woman was standing on the balcony— probably the Egyptian "nanny" as they called her. I had heard about her two years ago, though I had never seen her. She, too, had learned that there was a fellow Egyptian in Abu Amer's villa, as one of the Pakistanis once informed me. In fact, not that long ago, when she heard that I was about to go home on vacation, she had one of the Pakistani maids in her villa ask one of the Pakistani maids in Abu Amer's villa to ask me whether I would take some things back to her family in Cairo. I relayed back a message saying that I would. On the plane I had an extra suitcase full of clothes, an envelope with some cash in it, and a letter, and a small velvet-covered box containing a gold chain and earrings. She had written the amount of cash on the outside of the envelope in a small meticulous script.

She motioned me toward the front gate. Having not yet made up my mind whether to meet up with the others, I obeyed her gesture. The gate swung open as I approached. A gravel path, lit by the low footpath lights, led to the main entrance. By the time I reached the three steps up to the front door landing, she had opened the door.

"Please come in," she said as she turned to go inside. I followed.

I found myself in a vast entrée with dozens of chairs and subdued lighting in the corners. She was in a purple dressing gown with a scooped neckline. I placed her around forty. Her hair was gathered to one side and she twiddled the ends with one hand as she indicated something with the other. Eventually I realized that she meant the couple of armchairs that had been obscured by the shadows.

I was rebuking myself for having accepted her invitation when she said, "You don't like the place?" She smiled and tilted her head. "I don't either. It's way too big."

She led the way to a glass-enclosed balcony containing a couch and two chairs. It overlooked a portion of the garden in which there were stunted palms, many red and yellow rose bushes, and some chairs and tables here and there. "This is my favorite place in the villa," she said. "I sit in here and just let my mind wander until she calls for me to come up to her."

Her voice was so close that I felt it would be too awkward to look in her direction. She said, "Relax. There's no one else here. They've all gone out. I was about to, too, but then I thought, where would I go? My job is to sit and keep her company. That's what I've grown used to. I don't know anybody outside these grounds. I've seen you three or four times from this balcony. I wanted to speak with you but I couldn't figure out how. Then the soccer match came. So now, tell me."

We were on the couch, our shoulders almost touching. Seeing my confusion she said, "When you were back in Egypt you saw my family. You haven't told me about them yet."

"That was almost a year ago."

"That's right, a year. But how could I speak with you? All you said in your letter was that they were fine. It's been six years since I've seen my husband and daughter. She must be all grown up now. Did you see her?"

"Yes."

"Does she look like me?"

I turned toward her to make the comparison and was sur
prised to find her face so close to mine. Her eyes sparkled.
I straightened my back, pointed my knees straight in front
of me and turned my attention to the garden again. I always
avoided this type of situation. I'd heard too many stories to
drop my guard: fifty lashes in a public flogging and expul-
sion, without collecting one's outstanding pay or receiving
the end-of-service bonus stipulated in the contract. How
many of such cases had there been during my five years here?
Seven involving Arab workers. Their assignations had been
arranged so cautiously that it was a wonder they could ever
have been exposed. The walls must have had ears. A nurse or
a waitress would go out shopping. After entering one of those
enormous malls, wandering in and out of various stores and
eventually emerging, like many others, with several shopping bags, she would take the bus to the old town. She would
then make her way to one of those densely populated build-
ings with men and women coming and going all the time and,
there, she would meet her lover. How could they have been
discovered? The more I thought about this the greater my
conviction grew that eyes were everywhere. The seven cases
had a major element in common. They all involved relatively
new arrivals; they had been in the Emirate for no more than
a few months. Their blood was still warm; they had not yet
made the adjustments the rest of us had. Somewhere along
the line in my five years here I had shut a door—"the door
that lets in the wind," as we say back home. Or maybe the
door simply shut by itself. Nothing excites me anymore. Not
a beautiful body strutting its hips—and there's no shortage
of that here. Not a pair of nicely rounded legs, their smooth

31

glowing skin peaking from beneath a skirt as they swing into a car. I avert my eyes and pick up my pace. I notice nothing.

There was this man who worked as a driver for an Emirati family. Fresh from the Philippines; he didn't last more than two weeks. As the story was told to me, every time he opened the car door for his employer's wife, he would ogle her legs as she lifted them into the car. He got off easy: they simply terminated his contract. He wept as he toted his suitcase to the airport. "After all the money I spent to come here . . . . If only they'd tell me why," he moaned to his companions. They knew why, of course, having listened to him talking about his job. But they did not reveal to him his transgression. "The least we could do was to let him return home as innocently as he came," they explained.

I had been here about two years when I heard this story. Afterward, from my place in the garage, I observed the Filipino driver as he let Umm Amer or her daughters into the car. He'd been here a year and a half longer than I had. He stood stiffly, gripping the handle and staring down at his shoes until the women settled into their seats, then he closed the door and let himself into the driver's seat.

That day I thought, "They're right, of course. Who'd want a driver who ogled his wife's or daughters' legs? In fact, how can a man feel sure that his house and womenfolk are safe after discovering that one of his employees had betrayed his trust?" Such were the thoughts that came to mind again and again upon hearing of each of those seven cases, which seemed to occur at three- or four-month intervals. "They're right," I'd think. "The guy who does it with some working girl today could do it with an Emirati woman tomorrow. Once you get used to something it's hard to stop." And so I would say to

32

others, sometimes adding the caution, "The doors of tempta-
tion once opened . . ." along with the advice: "It's easy All you
have to do is resolve to forget, and you'll find you've forgotten.
Dead coals don't glow and don't burn those who touch them."

Those who'd hear this would nod and say, "How right you
are."

"Yes, and after all," I'd say, "our bosses trust us and treat
us well."

Within a few months I succeeded in putting sex out of my
mind. I simply pretended women did not exist or, rather,
I learned to look at them the same as men. When I would
do the occasional before-and-after comparison of myself I
would find that nothing crucial had been lost. Just a few minutes worth of orgasm. These I made up for in my dreams. I
would wake up and feel the moisture on my groin. As always,
the dream involved my wife. I would feel relieved and go back
to sleep with no worry but the need to shower and wash my
pajamas in the morning.

Sometimes as I sat in front of the garage contemplating what I had become, I would reassure myself: in spite of
everything, in the five years I've been here I managed to save
up enough money to build a two-story house in my village.
I would catch sight of the Pakistani maids, hastening in and
out of the kitchen and bustling after their chores. They're like
me, I'd think. They must have gone through the same change.
Once, in the course of my ruminations in front of the garage,
I flashed back to what the farmers in my village do when a
bull goes on the rampage. Occasionally a bull goes wild, starts
butting and kicking the other animals and then leaps onto a
female with such force that he nearly lacerates her. Sometimes
it is so blinded by its sexual frenzy that it will go for anything

on four legs. In order to restore peace and quiet in the herd, the farmers either castrate or slaughter it.

I had never asked for a holiday, although I was owed one. I was afraid to see my wife. I kept telling myself that the day would come when I would be whole again. Not that I have some illness or am worn out from work. As they say in the coffeehouses in the old town, people can change from one day to the next. And from one place to the next: you can be whole on the roof and half a man in the bedroom.

But one day Abu Amer took me by surprise. "I've noticed that you haven't asked for a vacation like the rest of them. You're owed four years' leave. Don't you miss your family?"

His voice was friendly and his eyes were smiling. After some hesitation I said, "Whatever you say, Abu Amer."

"A whole month. You deserve it. Make your arrangements and let me know."

When I got home, I surprised myself. The moment I stepped through the door and saw the thrill on my wife's face as she rushed up to hug me, I was filled with an overwhelming surge of lust.

The nanny led me through the corridors of the villa. She told me her name was Zahiya and that she'd been here six years and had nothing to complain of. Her slender figure swayed slightly as she walked ahead of me. Her name suited her; she was "splendid." She often dreamed of her family, she said, though she didn't dream often. Her husband was a decent and honest man. He was a good husband and had never harmed her in any way. She and her daughter were everything to him. As their daughter grew and her needs increased—for clothes and the like—he tried to find a job abroad, but without

34

success. So he said to Zahiya, "Why don't you give it a try. You'll have a better chance." And she did.

She said, "I've asked for leave time and time again. They get used to you here. Eventually I gave up asking."

As she walked, a sheer pink nightgown peeped out beneath the hem of her dressing gown. I tried to keep my eyes averted. It revealed the beginnings of her long legs. They were beautiful as they bent and straightened with each graceful step she took. She had advertised her desire clearly enough. What worried me was what would come next. I followed her leadenly, lagging a little behind as I tried think up an excuse to leave. She didn't give me a chance. She kept up a running commentary as we passed from room to room, explaining that we were now in a small screening room or remarking on the paintings on the wall. "This villa's pretty much the same as yours. They were built at the same time. When they were younger, Abu Amer and Abu Salem were bosom buddies. You wouldn't see one without the other. Now they rarely see each other. They're too busy with their businesses and the like."

She talked endlessly about Umm Salem. "My job is to keep her company. Umm Amer visited her twice. I saw her both times. She's a kind and pretty woman, but difficult. I didn't like her. Umm Salem didn't take to her either. I wonder what's going to happen while they're staying in the same hotel in France. How long is the match going to last anyway?"

I said I didn't know.

"Here's her room."

She stood at the open door and waited for me to catch up. I stopped a yard or so away. She smiled and said, "Have you ever seen her?"

"How could I?"

She laughed. "Are you afraid? I mean of Umm Salem? Have you ever seen such a large bed?"

The bedroom was as large as a living room. The bed was right in the middle, big enough to accommodate four people stretched out comfortably with space in between. A heavy curtain hung over the sliding door to the balcony. Through an open door, on one side, I glimpsed the edges of a mirror and a sink. There was another door in the room but it was closed. A huge television was mounted on the wall facing the bed. Below it were several glass shelves holding three decoders and a video player. A small refrigerator stood next to the bed. Several remote control devices of different shapes and sizes lay on top.

Zahiya placed a knee on the mattress and leaned over to adjust the pillows. I took in the subtle undulations of her back, the curve of her hips, the plump naked flesh of her calves . . . and I was not aroused. She stood up. Her dressing gown had fallen open, the ends of the belt falling to either side. Her sheer pink nightgown shimmered in the bedroom light. She had nothing on beneath it to conceal her belly, her navel, her dark areolas. I discovered her eyes waiting for mine to meet hers again. I looked away. She gathered her dressing gown together again and tied the belt. Her movements were unhurried and leisurely; she was obviously enjoying her display.

"Everything's within reach from here. She doesn't even have to leave her bed except to go to the bathroom, which is only a couple of steps away, as you can see. She's incredibly fat. She lies on her back with her legs spread out—they're so fat that she can't bring her feet together. The doctors abroad advised her to have her intestines shortened, but she refused. 'What's wrong with food? It's nice,' she says."

Zahiya gathered her hair together into a thick bundle, folded it, and pinned it to the top of her head.

"Umm Salem was slender when she first married, but her husband told her, 'Your bones hurt me.' So she started to eat. She ate and ate and grew fatter and fatter. She couldn't control herself. Abu Salem hardly ever comes up here anymore. He stays out in the garden and then disappears. They scour the grounds for him but can't find him. Once in a while they'll come across him on a couch in one of the living rooms. He has a separate bedroom downstairs. I don't know why he doesn't go there instead of sleeping on the couch. He often has friends over for dinner and then goes out with them. Anyway, they hired me to keep his wife company. She was lonely and had no one to speak with. She couldn't understand the Filipino and Pakistani maids. Their English was too broken. They asked her whether she wanted a Syrian or Lebanese companion and she said, 'No, I want an Egyptian.' She always watches Egyptian serials on television, so she said it had to be an Egyptian. This is my chair." She indicated the armchair near the bed. "Try it out. It's comfortable."

She laughed and said, "The very first day she asked me all about myself and my husband and daughter. From then on, she did all the talking. She talked and talked, and I listened. Whenever I tried to amuse her with some story or other, she'd listen a bit then interrupt me and pick up her story where she left off. She wouldn't even pay attention to the comments I made. So eventually I learned to just keep my mouth shut and listen. Often she'd forget what she told me and end up repeating it a week later . . . about her father, her mother, her childhood. There were two boys—cousins of hers—she used to play with when she was about ten.

They were in love with her and she was in love with them. Both of them; she couldn't be with one without the other. If one of them was late, she'd make the other go out with her to fetch him. She'd always take one of them off into some corner or room," Zahiya chuckled. "I mean if you could see her face light up when she talks about her childhood. She returns to it night after night. The other stories eventually fade, but not these. Once, her mother caught her in one of the bedrooms cuddled up with one of the boys. The mother wrenched the boy out of the bed and started giving him a thrashing. The girl screamed and tried to free him from her mother. Her mother kept pushing her away, so she bit her—sank her teeth into her mother's arm. Her mother turned on her. Such a thrashing; she had never experienced anything like it before or after. Her father kept her housebound after that and forbade any boy visitors; only girls were allowed. Ah, every woman in the world has stories from her childhood, but they forget. Why would they remember? But Umm Salem . . . ."

Zahiya shook her head sadly. She was sitting on the edge of the bed with one leg crooked beneath her. From time to time she would lightly scratch her shiny knee with her fingernails. I sat facing her, slouched in her chair.

"She talks non-stop and I listen. I say, 'Should I make you a cup of coffee with milk?' She loves coffee. But she says, 'Not yet,' and goes on talking. The boy who got a smacking from her mother swallowed some poison or some pills that day. He had to be rushed to hospital. Umm Salem went crazy when she heard the news. She climbed down a tree outside her balcony—got scratches all over her face and body—and walked all the way to the boy's house. When the boy's mother opened the door, she just stood there, scratches and dried blood and all, without saying a word. The good woman took her inside and washed her face, arms, and legs before taking her in to see her son. The other boy was there.

"After the mother had left them, she said to the boy in bed, 'I'm mad at you.' When he didn't answer, she said again, 'I'm mad at you. Why didn't you tell me you were going to kill yourself? If you'd told me, we could have committed suicide together. We could have gone off to some secret place and killed ourselves together.'

"The other boy accompanied her home. On the way, she broke down. She buried her head on his chest and wept while he patted her on her back until she calmed down. She asked him, 'What about you?'

He said, 'I don't like suicide.'

"She remembers all that as if it happened yesterday. She tells me every single detail—what they ate, what they drank. I asked her, 'What happened to the boys?'

"She sighed and said, 'Oh, they went abroad. One went to London and the other—the one who tried to commit suicide—went to America. He comes back on holidays to see his family. I always hear about it when he comes, with his wife and kids, and I wonder whether he remembers that girl he almost killed himself over. He can't have forgotten. He must have asked about me and learned that I'm married now, too. If I weren't the way I am now, I'd ask him to come over and visit. Sometimes I picture us meeting. I'd be as slender as I was before I got married. We'd hold hands and neither of us would speak; we'd just look at each other. I never saw him again after that day when I heard of his suicide attempt. Maybe it was because they were so worried about him that his parents packed him off to some relatives of his in America where he finished his schooling. He wrote to me three months after he got there. My mother intercepted the letter—I saw my name on the envelope. She opened it and read it standing up. She didn't say a word; just threw me an angry stare. I snuck behind her when she went to her bedroom, so I saw where she hid it. When she came back into the living room and saw me she said, "His mother's going to be getting that letter today." Afterward, when she went to fetch the letter and couldn't find it, she called me into her room. "Did you take that letter?" she asked. "Yes," I said. I could feel my face burning. "And where is it?" "I tore it up." Her eyes bored into mine. She knew I was lying. But she sent me out of the room without saying another word. The boy never wrote to me again.'"

"At that point Umm Salem gave me a wistful smile then turned her face away. After a long silence, she said, 'Over there in the jewelry box. You'll find it beneath the lining of the cover. I haven't read it in a long time.'

"I followed her directions. What a state that piece of paper was in! I was afraid I'd tear it just by pulling it out of its hiding place. I handed it to her. She unfolded it gently and shifted her body up a bit so she could read: "'*My beloved* . . . .'"

"That's all she read out loud. She ran her eyes lovingly over the paper. Then she refolded it along its creases and said, 'Put it back.'

"I was perplexed. It looked like she had wanted to read the letter to me. What changed her mind? Did she want to keep something in it secret? But she'd confided so many secrets in me. Anyway, I told myself, that's her business."

Zahiya rose and adjusted her dressing gown. She went over to the dressing table, took hold of a large dish of nuts and placed them before me. She asked me whether I would like something to drink. I shook my head.

She resumed her seat on the bed and said, "I bathe her twice a day. Once in the morning and once before she goes to sleep. I rub her body with talcum powder and spray her bed with jasmine scent—also twice a day. If she hears her husband come home she asks me to bathe her again. Then I help her get made-up, prop her up on the pillows and leave the room. But Abu Salem doesn't come up here. He stays downstairs with his friends until he leaves again, with them. When I first came to work here he was called Yasser and she was called Khadija. Their son, Salem, wasn't even a dream yet. Anyway, eventually she calls me back and asks, 'Has he gone out?' When I tell her he has she says, 'Adjust me so I can sleep.' Once I get her comfortable she drops off to sleep."

Zahiya pointed to the closed door. "That's my room. She rings for me at night to help her go to the bathroom. There's a buzzer attached to the headrest on my bed. It's really shrill. When it goes off I nearly hit the ceiling. It takes a while before my heart stops pounding and I realize where I am. Then she rings a second time. That means I'd better hurry because she can't hold it in anymore."

She fell silent. A languor had crept into her posture and her voice. But there was a tinge of sorrow, as though she was on the verge of broaching something unpleasant. I readied myself to listen. Her head was bowed. She had secured the folds of her dressing gown so that now not even a hint of the pink nightgown was visible.

"When I saw you I felt I had to speak with you. I have no one here I can talk to. You're from my own country and you've met my family. I thought that by speaking with you I might be able

41

to feel a little less homesick. But all I've spoken about was her. I didn't say what I planned to say. Now I don't know if I will."

I was thrown by her sudden withdrawal, especially after the way she had come on to me at first. Perhaps she sensed my distance. Or maybe she had heard the rumors about what happens to foreign workers here, thought that as a man from her country I would be immune, and decided to put me to the test. Then, when she didn't get the reaction she had expected, she gave up and changed her attitude toward me. But I was not convinced. More likely, she was being perfectly natural. After all, I wasn't exactly a stranger in her eyes. Familiarity is relative: there's a bond between fellow countrymen abroad that doesn't exist back home. I was inclined to believe her. She had something to tell me about herself, but whenever she started to speak she found herself talking about the other woman. As I waited for her to speak again, I contemplated her beautiful face, which was angled to one side.

Eventually she said, "Maybe another time, if you'd care to drop by."

I stood up. She watched me for a moment then said, "You too. You're a listener." She smiled apologetically. "You haven't said a word about yourself. I haven't even asked you about yourself." She smoothed down the wrinkles on the front of my thawb. "I'll open the door for you."

She led me to a panel of buttons on the wall outside the bedroom and pushed one. Through the window I could see the outside gate swing open. That was the window where I had seen her standing when I was doing my rounds earlier that evening.

8

The lights startled me. They had slipped my mind. Thousands of brilliant colors burst in the sky and expanded into huge crystalline balloons, which merged to form a glittering ceiling over the Emirate. All the shops were still open and brightly lit. The sidewalks were packed with pedestrians who, like me, paused at the sound of a mounting roar. Within seconds the source came into view. A huge crowd jammed into the far end of the street. It was a medley of different nationalities—Pakistanis, Indians, Filipinos, Sudanese, Arabs—most in their native dress, carrying Emirati flags and pictures of the Emirati soccer team and waving and cheering. I was unable to make out the words to many of their songs and chants. The parading revelers kept spaces clear for groups of dancers. A troupe of Sudanese passed by, their white jallabiyas billowing and huge turbans bobbing as they swayed back and forth, clapping to the rhythm of beating drums. The Indians followed, their procession led by a row of men in knee-length tunics, thick mustaches greased and coiled, and jewels glittering in their colorful turbans. They held themselves erect, chests puffed

43

out, as they marched with their arms interlocked, as though acting as a dam to stem the gush of the throng. Their fellow countrymen behind them carried a bed of nails upon which sat the immemorial Hindu aesthete. Closely resembling Gandhi, his short cotton dhoti reached to his knees and his emaciated legs were interlocked in the lotus position. Next came the Filipinos, chatting and laughing as they ambled along as though on a picnic outing. Because of their diminutive height their segment of the procession seemed like a dip in a road. The Arabs, who came next, wore everything from jallabiyas to suits and ties. An Egyptian carried on others' shoulders was the most zealous cheerer in their segment of the parade. "With our soul, with our blood we support you!" he bellowed, pausing to let the others echo the chant after him, fists punching the air. I joined in from where I was standing, clapping to the beat of the chant. In the distance I could see the stadium lights glittering. That must be where they were heading.

No sooner had the procession turned the corner than another appeared at the other end of the street. Marching to the accompaniment of tabla drums and reed flutes, they carried colorful banners and placards with photos of the national team. I decided to go to the stadium too. But first I wanted to check up on the situation back at the villa. Also, I thought, maybe some of the others there would like to come along.

Four of the Pakistani women were sitting in a small circle in front of their quarters. They beckoned me over. There was no sign of the Filipinos. Rishim and her husband were seated next to each other near the garden gate. A large tray bearing coffee and tea implements had been placed on a low table in front of them. They were speaking in low confidential voices in the soft glow of the lawn lights.

"He wants to leave," one of the women told me.

In response to my surprise and confusion, they averted their faces and shot their hands up to cover their awkward smiles. Suddenly it clicked. They were cannier than I had thought. For the longest time they've been watching the Filipinos and me going about our errands and joking around as though we didn't have a care in the world while they—the women—didn't betray the slightest hint that they were aware of our condition. There flashed to mind the many times I had to drop by their quarters in the mornings to speak to them about some household business. Often one of them would come to the door, still in her slip and holding the dress that she was about to put on, seemingly oblivious that her shoulders and parts of her breasts were bared. Since I knew that they were not the flirtatious type, I read nothing into their behavior apart from the fact that they were in a hurry and regarded us as akin to brothers.

I stared blankly at the ground as I thought this through. Then I nodded to the couple in their adjacent chairs. "And him? What's the matter with him? She's his wife. What's he afraid of?"

I was about to head in their direction to find out, but the four women supplied the answer:

"He didn't bring a nightshirt and he wouldn't use one of Abu Amer's and he refused to sleep in little Amer's bed."

"Rishim came to us in tears. She didn't know what to do."

"Yeah, she told us everything."

"So we said, 'At least he should stay with you for these few days, because he won't be able to see you or speak with you again after they come back from France.'"

"But she said that he told her that he had missed her and that he was happy just to have seen her. He keeps insisting that it's too dangerous for both of them if he stays here."

"Why does he think it's dangerous?" I asked.

"That's what we asked her. She said she didn't know."

"Why didn't the four of you go sit with them? Maybe that would have helped him relax."

"We were going to at first, but then we thought we should leave them alone together for the first day."

"Then, after Rishim told us what happened we thought we'd better ask her first. She went off to speak with him again. When she came back she told us that he wanted to leave."

"Maybe it would help if you sat with him a bit," suggested another.

"What would I talk to him about? If he wants to leave, let him leave."

9

The streets had emptied; everyone was at the stadium taking part in the festivities, no doubt. The stores were still open but had few shoppers. The staff, themselves, had left—probably to the stadium, too. I went into a shop and spotted a sign that read, "Please help yourself and leave the money next to the cash register." I took a pack of cigarettes off the shelf and a box of candy that I am fond of. I dropped a bill in the box next to the cash register and extracted the change. There was also a candy jar filled with coins, just in case the exact change wasn't available in the box. This was not unusual. Stores here also stay open and unstaffed at prayer times, with the same sign displayed and similar arrangements for payment.

A Syrian gentleman behind me said to his companion, "As you can see, their trust in their customers is boundless. They have hidden cameras that can pick up a cockroach moving—if they have cockroaches here. What they do with the videotapes themselves I have no idea. They can only serve as memorabilia. Only a fool would think he could make off with a fortune, because before he knew it he'd be watching himself on film caught red-handed."

As I turned to leave I offered the gentlemen a polite smile. They returned the gesture.

"Syrian?" I asked, simply because I felt like saying something.

"Lebanese," he answered, even though his accent was unmistakably Syrian.

I smiled again and left.

Speaking of trust, I later learned that the Indian officers in the police stations released most of their detainees on strict orders that they report for roll call every morning and return to their cells the day before the Emiratis were due back. These inmates were only up for petty crimes such as brawling or insolence toward their superiors.

I wandered through the vacant streets trying to make up my mind. I wanted to go to the stadium, but decided that it was too far to walk. There were no cars to hitch a ride with, but nor did I feel like returning to the villa in order to fetch one of Abu Amer's cars. I was not in the mood to face the glumness there. I had few friends in the Emirate. The ones I had, lived in the old town, but they were all probably at the stadium anyway. Still, I thought, I haven't seen them for a long time. Maybe I should join them. It could be fun. We'd chat and laugh as we watched the celebrations. Maybe we'd even join in.

I found myself in front of Abu Salem's villa. I stopped and looked around, thinking I'd better get away from here. Zahiya—all the while she had been in the back of my mind. She was alone in the house. The rest of the ten or eleven domestics were out, most likely at the stadium, but she preferred to stay home. She hadn't said a word about them earlier. She probably has little to do with them because she's always with Umm Salem. She even sleeps in that adjacent bedroom.

Maybe that makes her feel a bit above the rest, so she refuses to socialize with them. Not that she seemed interested in going out. When she had finished talking, she looked like she merely wanted me to leave so she could be alone with her own thoughts. Apparently Umm Salem is all she thinks about, even when Umm Salem is away. Would she come with me to the stadium? Would she enjoy the excitement there? Hard to picture it. I walked back and forth in front of the villa. If she comes out on the balcony I'll ask her to come with me.

I heard the "psst" I'd been anticipating. I looked up to her balcony and saw her surreptitious signal. I slipped through the gate as it opened and headed up the long pathway between the hedges to the front door. She was standing on the landing smiling.

"I thought you might come back."

She took hold of my hand and led me inside. She was wearing an olive green dressing gown that hung open to reveal a yellow slip that halted at the knees. Her naked calves were beautiful. I watched them as I followed her, again, through the vast rooms and corridors, up the carpeted stairway and into Umm Salem's room. The dimmed lighting was relaxing. I automatically headed to her armchair. She smiled as she lifted her hair to the top of her head, exposing her graceful white neck, and took up her cross-legged position on the bed.

"I thought you might be asleep," I said.

"I did sleep a bit, but I woke up again. I don't sleep well when I'm alone. My mind starts wandering here and there and suddenly I find I'm wide awake."

"Do you miss her?"

"I've grown used to her. It's been so many years. Oh, I haven't told you yet . . . ." She shifted her legs and loosened

her robe a bit. Her face glowed. "She called me one night . . . .
I mean, she rang that buzzer on my bedstead . . . . Oh! I
almost forgot!"

She leaped up, directing my attention to a corner of the
room where there was a table set with plates and covered
platters. "Have a bite to eat with me. I thought that if you
came back we'd have dinner together. So I waited."

She strode barefoot over the carpeted floor to the table. I
followed. Vegetable soup, slices of roast beef, a green salad.
I suddenly felt very hungry and dug in. She watched me
for a moment contentedly. Then she said, "I usually eat by
myself—in there." She pointed to her room. "They bring in
her tray first. I help her eat then I wipe her hands and mouth
with a moist cloth. Then they bring in my tray, which I take
into my room."

I finished my food and waited for her to finish hers. When
I started to rise, she gestured for me to stay seated, left the
room and returned with a bowl inlaid with mother-of-pearl,
containing scented water. In the custom of Emiratis after
they finish their meals, she dipped a hand cloth in the water
and handed it to me. I wiped my mouth and hands, stood up
and returned to the armchair. She cleared off the table and
returned after a short while with a small table bearing a ther-
mos of hot water and the makings of tea and coffee. As she
resumed her place on the bed, her robe fell open to reveal
the short slip. In spite of the amount of white thigh that
was exposed, I did not feel aroused. Curiosity, perhaps, or a
slight tingling of the thrill we men feel when glimpsing a bit
of female flesh. That was all.

"Should I read the coffee cup for you?" she offered.

"Which cup?"

She laughed. "The cup I read for her every night. 'See how it is with him,' she says, meaning her husband.

"'Everything's fine,' I tell her.

"'I know that,' she says. She trusts him, even after he stopped coming up here. She always manages to find an excuse for him. It would never even occur to her that he might want to take a second wife. She's from an important family and he made a lot of his investments using her money. Not that she would tell me this outright. I gathered it from the stories she tells me about their first years of marriage."

Zahiya poured the tea and handed me a cup. She stared for a moment into the steam rising from her tea then set the cup on the little table.

"There was this night she rang for me. I had just bathed her an hour earlier. So when the buzzer went off I was a bit alarmed. When I went into her room I found the bedside lamp on and her head propped up on her elbow, eyes wide open. This was unusual for that time of night. She stared at me for a moment and then said, 'Yasser's here.'

"'I haven't heard him.'

"'Me neither.'

"I sniffed the air in the direction of her bedroom door, which was open. There wasn't a trace of that powerful cologne that always wafts around him.

"'You won't smell it,' she said, 'He didn't put any on tonight. He did that on purpose so that I wouldn't know he's here. My intuition never lies. Go downstairs and see what he's up to.'

"I was in my nightgown so I started to head back to my room.

"'Where are you going?'

"'To put on my dressing gown.'

51

"She did this flick of her hand she does whenever she's annoyed or disgusted. It really irritates me but I always forgive her. Anyway, that flick made me stop in my tracks. She narrowed her eyes at me and said, 'What's wrong with you? Go put on your dressing gown—as if it would make any difference.'

"She looked away. My face must have gone bright red. I'd gone rigid in the effort to fight back my tears. But seconds later she turned back and started eying me up and down. What had come over her? She's like that. Sudden mood swings. Usually I play along, but this time I wasn't going to let her get away with it. I was going to give her a piece of my mind. I was furious. She was still scanning every inch of my body. She leaned her head to the side so she could see my rear then her eyes climbed upward and stopped at my breasts. I was squirming beneath her stare. I folded my arms across my breasts and just stood there not knowing what to do. The movement of my arms must have brought her to her senses. She looked me straight in the eyes, nodded toward my bedroom and said, 'Go put on your dressing gown.'

"I felt this sudden sense of relief. But when I looked back on it later, I realized that everything that has happened since began at that moment. I blame myself. If only I'd reacted differently then. Whatever was going on in my head?

"Anyway, I put on my dressing gown and went down to the first floor. I stayed barefoot so no one could hear me coming. There are three guestrooms down there. The door to one of them was closed. After walking back and forth a bit, I stopped and paused at the door. There was only a faint whispering, but I could make out his voice. I went back upstairs.

"'Who's with him?' she asked.

"'I don't know.'

"'Was it a woman's voice, or a man's?'

"'I didn't hear the other voice.'

"'But you heard Yasser.'

"'I didn't hear what he said. I just recognized the sound of his voice.'

"'The sound of his voice? Huh!' Her eyes darted around the room, then she said, 'Go back down there and find out who's with him.'

"'How am I supposed to do that?'

"'Put your ear to the door.'

"'What if he opens it?'

"'He's not going to open it. But even if he does, tell him I sent you.'

"'He wouldn't believe me.'

"'Okay, open the door as though by accident and take a look.'

"'What if one of his friends is with him? What would that look like? Don't make me do something that would cause trouble.'

"'What trouble would that cause?'

"Then she fell silent and leaned back on her pillows. After a moment she said, 'There's an armchair on the other side of the column in front of that room. Crouch in that chair and wait till they come out.'

"'What if they stay in there until the morning?'

"'I'm sure it's a woman. She'll be leaving long before the night's out. I know Yasser. Once he's finished with her he'll get her out of there as quick as he can.'

"There was no way I could win with her. He's her husband. She knows him better than I do.

"So I went back downstairs, curled myself up in that armchair and pulled my robe around me because that hall's cold and drafty. I was scared that I would fall asleep. In fact, I was just about to nod off when I heard the door handle click. He came out first. The woman behind him was adjusting her overcoat. It had a hood, but I caught a glimpse of her before she slipped it over her head. She was blond, young, and very pretty. I knew Khadija was going to ask me for every detail, so I took a good look at her, waited until I heard the front door shut behind them and went back upstairs.

She was sitting up with her back against the pillows and her enormous legs flopped out to either side. Her eyes were glowing with excitement; I couldn't believe it. She put her finger to her lips then gestured toward the little side table, the electric kettle, and the dressing table. I brought over things she indicated— the bowls of candy and nuts—and made her a cup of Nescafé. Then she patted the mattress next to her leg, indicating where I should sit. Only after I sat did she speak: 'Now, tell me.'

"I told her what I saw. As I'd expected, she asked me to describe the woman. After I did, she had me describe her again. As I spoke, she popped one piece of candy after the other into her mouth, keeping her eyes fixed on my face the whole while. When I finished she said, 'An import. Hand me the washcloth.'

"I handed her the moistened washcloth then, after she wiped her mouth and hands, she explained, 'She's a nurse from the hospital. The director's a pimp. He hires them from Europe and Australia. They'd probably never worked as nurses a day in their lives before then. He performs this service for important men in the Emirate, which is why he's held on to his job so long. Have you heard about this already?'

"'What I hear I don't tell.'

"'Oh yeah, I forgot.'

"As though thinking out loud, she said, 'What surprises me is that he brought her here. He's got an apartment in the suburbs. He's taken several women there, so why not this one? What do you think?' Not expecting an answer, she continued, 'Maybe it's because she's from Europe and it's his first time with her and he wanted to impress her with the villa and the luxury. Who knows? If only you'd caught a bit of what they talked about then I might understand. You wouldn't be keeping something from me would you?'

"'How could I hear anything? The chair's too far away from the door.'

"'What about as they were leaving? Not a word?'

"'Not a word.'

"She stared at me for a moment, her eyes still glowing. Suddenly she asked, 'Who chose your name—Zahiya?'

"'My mother, I think.'

"'May God keep her in good health.'

"'She died a long time ago.'

"'Even so.' She pointed to the side table and said, 'Take that away and stretch me out.'

"When I had her settled in her sleeping position, she gave a long sigh and closed her eyes. But as I bent over to pick up the side table, she said, 'I don't know if I've told you yet. When I was crying my heart out on the chest of that young boy—mark this, I say *boy*, never either of their names—he put his arm around me, pulled me closer, and whispered soothing words. I was crying so hard that I wasn't aware of his hand on my back at first. But then I felt it inching down my spine. I'd never let either of the boys touch me before, apart from

55

some innocent kisses. But that day, even though I'd calmed down a bit, I kept crying and his hand kept going lower and lower. It was as though I was afraid that if I stopped crying, his hand would stop moving . . . . Oh, turn off the light. I'll tell you another time.'"

Zahiya paused and stared at the spot where the end of her dangling dressing gown belt had coiled on the floor. When she next spoke, it was as though from far away, "So I switched off the light."

After a moment's silence, Zahiya asked me whether I wanted something to drink. I didn't reply and she didn't ask again. She seemed tired and I sensed that her invitation to a drink was actually a hint to leave. I observed her as I made ready to stand up. The radiance in her face had begun to fade like a kerosene lamp running out of fuel. She gathered the end of the belt and placed it next to her on the bed. The lights outside flashed against the windowpane casting flickers of color on the bedspread. She absentmindedly snatched at them with her hand.

"They're shooting off fireworks," she said softly. After a brief silence she said, "We used to do that on feast days when we were little."

"Do you want to go out and watch the celebrations?"

"Go out?" Her voice rose as though the idea struck her as peculiar. She had grown rather pale and I was just about to ask her whether she was feeling ill when she said, "Sometimes talking wears me out."

"Has everyone else gone out?"

"Uh-huh."

"How about you?"

"Why would I go out? I have everything I need right here and I can see the fireworks from the balcony. Even when I

56

felt like I needed to talk with someone you came along." She looked at me kindly, her hands folded between her legs. "This time I was going to speak about myself. Even before I saw you I thought, 'If he comes back, I'll talk about myself. I've talked enough about her.'"

I stood up. She watched me for a moment from where she sat. Then she, too, rose to her feet as she said, "I don't know. Maybe I did speak about myself in a way."

She led the way into the corridor and pushed the button on the panel as I headed down the stairs.

10

walked down the empty street in the direction of the stadium. It was now past midnight. The stores had pulled down their shutters and the villas lay in darkness, apart from the dim lights on their front gates. I figured the festivities would go on for another two or three hours, which would leave time for the merrymakers to take a short rest before reporting to work at nine. A bus approached and pulled to a stop next to me even though I hadn't waved it down. I got in. Pakistanis and Sudanese were singing, in their own languages, their fingers drumming the rhythms on the backs of the seats in front of them.

The stadium was so full that the overflow spread up the slopes around the outer walls. Everyone who was left in the Emirate must have been there. Still, I found that I could make my way easily through the crowds, which by unspoken agreement had kept twisting corridors open between their large clusters. I wove through the babble of languages toward the stadium, inhaling the aromas of cuisines from around the world as I passed one food stand after another surrounded by midnight snackers.

Above the bleachers, dazzling spotlights were trained on huge billboards carrying pictures of the Emirati soccer team. Down in the arena, three dancing troupes performed along-side each other. I was drawn first to the Indian dancers. The lead dancer had a huge snake coiled around her body. She held its head as she twirled slowly in front of a chorus of female dancers holding wreaths of flowers, their brightly colored saris—wrapped to leave their bellies exposed—shimmering in the light. The Indian orchestra sat cross-legged on the ground in a semicircle behind the dancers. In the press of Indian onlookers I noticed the Hindu aesthete, still on the bed of nails but now reclined on his side with the mouthpiece of a water pipe in his hand. I traced the snaking hose to a huge water pipe and a huddle of Indians tending a brazier of burning coals.

The Pakistani troupe—next to the Indian one—consisted only of men, heads crowned with green skullcaps embroi-dered with white Arabic calligraphy. They sang what seemed to be religious chants. Occasionally they would pause in their recitations to intone supplications and Quranic verses.

I moved to the Egyptian troupe which had attracted quite a crowd. It featured a buxom belly dancer in a shiny black gown covered with glittering sequins. A scarf had been rolled up and tied around her hips to accentuate their movement. Two drummers followed her around the floor. The one with the tabla was crouched down so low that he almost seemed to crawl; the second held himself tall and jangled and thumped his tambourine in the air. Their act was followed by the tra-ditional village stick dance: two male performers in jallabiyas circled each other to the accompaniment of reed flutes, wielding their long and heavy canes in a stylized duel.

The odors of food now stirred my appetite. I headed out of the stadium and began to scout for some fellow Egyptians to have a bite to eat with. Gatherings of Indians, Pakistanis, and other nationalities beckoned me to their food trays as I passed. I declined as I am not fond of very spicy food. I caught sight of some tents amid circles of low lights on the sand dunes a little ways off. These were obviously for those who preferred to keep their distance from the crowds. I spotted three men waving to me from there—my Filipino colleagues. I headed toward them.

One began to explain to me the reason why the tents had been set up so far away. They were occupied by the domestics from the big villas, he began. "And they don't want to mingle with the others," I said, completing the thought.

He gave a loud snort of mock contempt and doubled over laughing.

"The Filipino snort sounds likes a frog croaking," I said.

In his mixture of broken Arabic and English, he replied, "Egyptian understand half-half. You snort like cows. These are villa servants. They're going to spend the night here. They brought blankets and pots and pans with them. Everything they need. They're going to stay here as long as the games last. In the mornings, they'll go back and clean and swim in the swimming pools. Then they're going to prepare the food and bring it back here."

"What about the Pakistani women?"

"They're all here." He pointed to one of the tents.

"Even Rishim?"

"Yeah, her too."

"And her husband?"

"I didn't see him. Come on, let's go over there."

We were in the male section of the Filipino tents. The women's section was next door.

"I see you're staying with your country folk. Where're the Egyptian tents?" I asked.

"Why?"

"I miss Egyptian food."

"Don't worry. I'll get you some."

"From where?"

"I know where their tents are," he said as he headed off.

Four of the women from Abu Amer's villa along with other Pakistani women were gathered around some grills in front of the tents, cooking corn and chestnuts. I asked after Rishim. One of them frowned and nodded toward one of the tents. "In there. She doesn't want to speak with anyone." She took me aside and said, "She's afraid that he doesn't love her anymore. She says he must have found another woman. She knows the situation here as well as we do and we told her so. But there's no getting through to her. What's in her head is in her head. She says that at least he could have stayed with her while the Emiratis are away."

I wondered what was in her husband's head. Perhaps he feared that people would find out they were married, which would mean they had falsified their work and visa applications. Just as I opened my mouth to explain this I realized she probably already knew it.

We returned to the grills and I took a seat alongside the other women from Abu Amer's. The Filipino I had spoken with earlier reappeared carrying a pot, which he placed in front of me. "Egyptian eats Egyptian!" he said with a loud guffaw. The pot was filled with stuffed cabbage leaves and grilled lamb. One of the women reached in, pulled out a stuffed cabbage leaf and tasted it. At her expression of delight, the other women dug into the pot.

The Filipino laughed when he saw how quickly the pot had emptied and he disappeared again. Soon he returned carrying a much larger pot. In his wake followed an Egyptian woman of about forty carrying another large pot. She told me that since she had been unable to communicate with the Filipino she'd decided to come herself to see if we needed anything else. "We have okra stew, mulukhiya, and grilled chicken," she said.

"The stuffed vegetables are more than enough," I answered.

"There're some people at our place who know you. Why don't you drop by?"

"Some other night. The games will be going on for some time."

"They told me to tell you that they have apple-scented tobacco if you care to share a water pipe with them."

"Please thank them for me. I don't smoke. Where do you work?"

"In the Happiness Beauty Salon in Zone Two. How about you?"

"At Abu Amer's villa."

"I know it. Umm Amer's a sweet lady. They called me over once to do her and her daughters' hair. They were about to take a trip abroad." After chatting a bit with the Pakistani women she left.

I suddenly felt very drowsy. I went over to the Filipinos' tent to sleep. The last thing I saw before I closed my eyes was the enormous poster of the soccer team suspended from tall poles. It was rustling slightly in the wind, and I could still hear the jumbled ruckus of the crowds and the music. Just before I fell asleep a new sound entered the fray. Loud and strident, it came from finger cymbals. But their ring was familiar. They sounded like the type used by village bands back home. Where would they have found them here? I'd never seen them on sale, not even at the junk merchants. They must have brought them over from Egypt along with their other instruments. I strained my ears in an attempt to home in on the music the band was playing, but it was impossible amid the collective din of other folk bands from around the world. Only the high-pitched jangle of the finger cymbals rose above the rest. I wondered whether the players in the band were wearing the same khaki uniforms with red sashes and epaulets as they did back home. I yawned. I'll catch them another night, I thought as I dropped off to sleep.

My wife appeared to me. She was just as I saw her when I had arrived home on vacation. I had set my suitcases beside me on the floor as she rushed toward me. She was so embarrassed by her visible excitement that her eyes looked everywhere but at mine. She was in a sleeveless jallabiya, open at the neck and light enough to reveal the flexing of her smooth hips as she prepared to throw herself into my embrace. I was terrified that I wouldn't be able to satisfy her. But as soon as her body touched mine I sensed my desire course through me like a heady incense. It was as though a heavy fog had lifted. I stood still, afraid to move. How I had missed that moment of sensual exhilaration, that sweet overwhelming warmth that tingled like a drug. So powerful was this sensation that I wouldn't let go of my wife when she tried to shift the way she was standing. She settled into my embrace and clung to me. We spent the rest of the day in bed. From time to time, she would get up, put on her dressing gown and answer the door. I'd hear her apologize to relatives or neighbors, telling them that I was exhausted from my trip and sleeping. Then she'd close the door and come back to bed. I tried to get her to try on the sexy lingerie I'd bought her. She refused at first, shaking her head so vigorously that her shoulders moved with it. But she finally gave in. She put on the garments and modeled them for me, her face flushed and averted.

"These are scandalous!" she exclaimed in a horrified whisper. "Weren't you embarrassed when you bought them?"

It was one of my few amusements in the Emirate, standing in front of the shop windows displaying women's lingerie. I'd buy the skimpiest pieces and I'd by a lot, in different models and colors. At night, back in my room, I'd open the suitcase in which I kept the gifts I bought for my wife and empty it out. I'd pick up one article after the other, unfold it, and hold it up as I tried to picture my wife in it. Then I'd fold them all up again, lay them back in the suitcase and lock it.

I was awoken by a noise different to the one that had sent me to sleep. Perhaps it was the very difference that shook me awake. It was the sound of rumbling motors. I peeked outside the tent, squinting at the glaring light. The stadium was empty. Cleaning vehicles were now crawling on the tarmac outside the stadium walls and garbage men had spread out on the grounds collecting litter. The flaps of the tents had been opened for airing, exposing the bedding, suitcases, and bundles inside them. Everyone must have gone off to work.

One of my colleagues strolled up, buttoning up his trousers. "Good, you're awake. When I saw you sleeping like the dead, I thought I'd go take a leak and wash up before I woke you up." He crouched down next to me. "The rest have gone back to the villa. Let's go. The garage is waiting for you. You didn't clean it yesterday. The cars too."

We got up and headed back to the villa.

That afternoon I took the car out for a drive. Earlier, the women cleaned the villa and prepared dinner to take to the tents. Then they went swimming—we could hear their shouts and laughter from the garage where we were washing the cars. Afterward they sat in front of their quarters combing their wet hair.

The Filipinos informed me that they were not going to the stadium that evening. They had other plans. After a moment, one of them asked, "Why don't you ask us what our other plans are?"

"Okay, what are your other plans?"

"You know the Grand Café in the old town? The African's going to be there."

"Who's the African?"

He shot a look of amazement at the other two and turned back to me. "You really haven't heard of him?"

"No."

"You Egyptians confuse me. Just when I begin to think I understand you, I realize I don't. Everybody in this town knows who the African is. Everybody from everywhere else.

But you, you're in another world. He's the only one of the foreign workers in the Emirate who hasn't been hit by the curse. He's still healthy."

"What do you mean?"

"I've seen him with my own eyes."

I stopped cleaning the car and turned toward him. "You saw him with your own eyes?"

"Not just me. Lots of others have too. I'm not going to say another word, not after that look you gave me. If you want to see him, you can come with us."

"I suppose somebody's asked him how he managed to escape the curse?"

"All he says is that the drums in his head never stop."

"What country's he from?"

"Who knows? The jungle. Pouncing beasts. Monkeys in trees. Drums going boom, boom."

His two colleagues were watching us with grins on their faces. They obviously knew what he was talking about. I promised to meet them at the coffeehouse after evening prayers.

As I drove out of Abu Amer's villa, I looked up at Abu Salem's. The balcony was empty. I kept driving.

It was an ordinary working day in the city. The stores were open and the foreign workers in the Emirate were going about their business as usual.

I slowed the car as I passed the police station. I'd heard that the inmates preferred to spend the day outside, sprawled out on the lawn in the back of the jail. I craned my neck toward the trees in the yard there, but from my car window I could only spot a few stretched out legs, dark skinny calves exposed where jallabiyas had ridden up, rubber flip-flops on the ground next to them. The Indian officer in charge was standing in front of my car, hands on his hips. He glanced at me just long enough to check me out and dismiss me.

I parked the car and headed into the market. It was packed, the haggling intense. The vendors here were expert bargainers. The Filipino vendors most of all, and the women were just as tough as the men. I bought a shawl, Iranian bread, and Lebanese mixed nuts, as the Pakistani women back at the villa had asked me to.

Just as I was about to leave, I heard a radio blare out the announcement: "The first match of the national team will take place the day after tomorrow at 5:00 p.m. All employees will be given the afternoon off to watch the match. It will be projected on the screens at the stadium for those who wish to watch it there."

12

The Grand Café was unusually packed. Clumps of men had even gathered on the sidewalk in front of the open windows. The windows were almost at ground level and only kept from serving as doors by wrought iron railings. I craned my neck in search of the Filipinos and eventually spotted them inside, seated around a table near the front. They had obviously arrived early. I edged my way through the many men who had not been fortunate enough to find seats until I reached my coworkers' table. They had an empty chair between them, which they had reserved for me.

"This is the second time we're going to see him. The first was four months ago," they told me.

A small circle had been left clear in the middle of the coffeehouse. That was where the African was sitting. A table had been placed next to his chair, and he was drinking tea and smoking a narghile, idly blowing smoke rings as though indifferent to the hundreds of eyes trained on him from all sides. A coffeehouse boy squatted on the floor in front of him, rearranging the coals on his water pipe with a pair of tongs.

The African was very dark and very thin. Wearing a white, collarless, wide-sleeved jallabiya, he had a little pointed goatee and frizzy salt-and-pepper hair. When he had had enough to smoke, he handed the mouthpiece to the coffeehouse boy who picked up the pipe and the empty glass of tea and headed to the kitchen. In moments the boy came back carrying a plate and a small plastic bucket of the kind that children play with at the beach.

The African stretched out his legs and crossed his ankles. His leather sandals had darkened and cracked. He pushed the plate a little toward the edge of the table and glared at his audience. The coffee boy returned again to place a glass of fenugreek tea on his table.

The standing members of the audience moved toward the table and, one-by-one, placed some money on the plate. Then those who were seated followed suit. When my turn came, I took a closer look. The odor of his sweat was pungent, in spite of the fan overhead. The skin on his face was dry, his lips were cracked, and he had a scar as long as a finger on the side of his neck. I returned to my seat disappointed not to have detected anything particularly unique.

He sipped slowly at his fenugreek tea until everyone returned to their places. Eventually the room fell silent. Only the whirring of the overhead fan could be heard. He set down his glass, leaned over to look at the plate and stirred the bills with his finger. Pressing his lips together, he leaned back in his seat, picked up his glass and took a long sip as he stared over the rim at the men at the windows. At that signal, they came in, placed their money on the plate and sat down cross-legged on the floor in front of the circle of tables.

The African pulled the plate toward him, collected the paper money, folded it and stuffed it in a pocket on the inside of his jallabiya. Then he lifted the plate, poured the coins into his hand and slipped them into an outside pocket.

He stood up and the coffee boy pulled his chair and table out of the way. The African pulled himself up to full height, took a deep breath, took two steps forward and one back and scanned his audience. Then he moved his feet slightly apart, snapped his fingers about half a yard in front of his crotch and emitted a high-pitched whistling sound from his mouth. He stood totally still with his eyes shut, as though concentrating on isolating himself from his surroundings. A moment or two passed. Then the fabric of the jallabiya began to quiver, almost imperceptibly at first. Like everyone around me I leaned forward and stared at the area intently. The whole room seemed to breathe in at once. The jallabiya rose slowly until it protruded like a tent. The African glanced down at it. He looked at his audience, turning his head as though to meet everyone's eyes. He hitched up his jallabiya and dropped his underpants and turned slowly in place. His member was huge. He knocked it with the back of his fingers. It sprang up and down and resumed its towering stiffness. The coffee boy reappeared with a glass of water and poured it into the pail. The African signaled for him to bring more. After the boy poured in a second glass of water, the African picked up the pail, hung it on his member and, again, turned slowly in place. He did this twice, all the while holding his head cocked to the side as though listening to a distant sound. Then he handed the pail to the coffee boy and pulled up his underpants. One of the customers rushed up with a chair. The African sat down, legs outstretched and his hands over his crotch, and closed his eyes.

The room remained silent, the audience still staring at him as though in a trance. Then, at the sound of someone clearing his throat, there was a rustling of movement and people began to get up, though still without uttering a word. As we filed out of the coffeehouse, many of us turned to take a last look at the African before we left. He remained in his chair, as motionless as the dead.

We thoughtfully made our way to our cars. When we reached them, one of the Filipinos said, "God is just. He chose an African. If he'd chosen any other nationality who knows what would have happened."

"The beating of drums does all that? Maybe it's those male potency pills we've been hearing about," said another.

"The curse is more powerful than those pills. Everyone here who's tried them has had no luck. I know, I'm one of them."

"But why did you even bother?"

"Just to see . . . . And I didn't see."

They asked me what I thought, this being my first time to have seen the performance.

"I don't know," I said. "I've never heard of anything like that before. I mean right out there in public in front of everybody. And without any feeling, as though he just pressed a button. Maybe it is the drumbeat, as you say."

"It sure is a miracle. History is full of miracles."

he stadium exploded in an ecstatic roar. After having watched the Emirate team win its first victory on the huge video displays, the crowds poured out of the stadium and streamed through the streets with a clamor of indiscernible cheers. This had to have been the first time in the history of the Emirate that women ever appeared in a march. Although they initially mingled with the rest, they soon spontaneously coalesced into their own separate segment.

I was in that crowd. By the time we neared Abu Amer's villa I felt too tired to go on. It was almost midnight. The parade had only just begun and still had many more streets to pass through, but I peeled off and headed home. As I passed by Abu Salem's place, I heard Zahiya's whispered call. I looked up, surprised that she was still up. She was on her balcony, but after seeing my head turn, she headed inside. The gate opened.

She stood at her usual place on the doorstep, clutching her dressing gown together with her hand. The ends of the belt were dangling on either side. I followed her into the reception hall. Although it was faintly lit, I could make out the dragon on the back of her green robe. These Chinese robes, which could be found in all the shopping malls, were a favorite among the foreign employees. They were affordable, attractive, and made nice gifts. Her nightgown was longer than the robe, reaching to her ankles. It was a light color and had an embroidered hem. At the foot of the stairs she stopped and turned to wait for me to catch up. Her robe was open enough that I could see the roundness of her belly and the dark circle of her navel through her clinging nightgown. I followed her up the stairs, taking in her pink-tinted heels and delicate ankles. Umm Salem's room .... The armchair next to the bed .... I was still amazed at how quickly I responded to her call, as though I had expected it. She smoothed down her hair and said, "I made dinner for you. Yesterday I did too. I waited but you didn't show up. The food's gone cold. I'll heat it up if you like."

"I was in the stadium. I ate something there. It's late. Maybe I should . . . ."

"It's not late at all. I sleep on and off. And the rest of the staff don't come home before dawn."

She had almost settled in her usual cross-legged position on the edge of the bed, but shot up again, saying, "Oh, I forgot!" She brought over the small coffee table and placed it next to my chair. Then she fetched the electric kettle and some cups. "I know you like your tea with two spoons of sugar."

She resumed her place. "I saw the soccer match too. I saw the Emir greet the members of the team. And Abu Salem, too. Did you see him?"

"I saw the Emir, but I didn't see him."

"He was sitting three rows behind the Emir, talking to the man next to him. Umm Salem didn't go of course. She can't take two steps without someone to prop her up. I don't even know why she went there at all. She'll be spending her whole time in bed in the hotel. She has Fatma there to help her. Fatma's a relative of hers and a friend from her schooldays. She's the one who convinced Umm Salem to go. She told her that she'd keep her company in the hotel whenever and for as long as she likes. You must be fed up with my talking about Umm Salem all the time."

"Not at all."

"I'm going to tell you something. You're from Egypt and you know my family. You'll tell me . . . ."

She turned to the window. A leafy branch of a tree hovered stilly not far from the other side of the windowpane.

"What I'm about to tell you . . . . I don't know."

Why was she so hesitant? Maybe she'd run out of things to say about Umm Salem.

She said, "This is the first time I've seen that branch with leaves on it. The shutters are always closed. Maybe I've seen it but forgotten."

She was not as energetic as the previous times I had been here. In fact, she looked somewhat pallid. "Alright, I'll tell you."

After a short pause she began, "Khadija called for me one day—that was how Umm Salem was called before she got married: Khadija. It was daytime. 'Get dressed,' she says.

"'Is everything alright?'

"'Get dressed. I'm going to send you on an errand.'

"I'd never left the villa before. This was the first time she'd ever sent me on an errand. I stood there a moment not knowing what to do. But then she gave me one of her dark looks, so I went back into my room and got dressed.

"When I came back in here, she said, 'Go to For Every Woman. I've already spoken with the people at the store.

74

They're expecting you. Pick out six Italian nightgowns and the underwear to go with them.'

"'But I already have enough nightgowns.'

"'I know. And pick out four light dressing gowns.'

"'I have enough of those too.'

"'I know. Now go. Oh! And get yourself a really nice French perfume. Any kind you fancy.'

"This was about a year after I got here. I went to the store, bought the items and came back. I left the package in my room, unopened. And she never asked to see what I brought.

"That evening she called me in here and said, 'Put on the pink nightgown and the black underwear beneath.'

"I had no idea what was going on. On my way back into my room she said, 'And do something with your hair.'

"That confused me even more. But I did as she told me to. When I came back, she said, 'That's it. Come a bit closer.'

"She examined me from head to toe. I could feel my face flush. The nightgown had thin shoulder straps and it was short—it went to just above my knees. She said, 'Very pretty. Very pretty. Now get *A Thousand and One Nights*.' I read those stories to her from time to time. After I fetched the book, she said, 'Read me a Sinbad story, any one of them.'

"She settled back onto her pillows and I sat at the edge of the bed next to her legs and started to read. I'm a bit shortsighted. I have to bring the book right up to my face and concentrate. Maybe that's why I didn't hear a sound at first. I read two pages and just as I was beginning the third I heard a soft cough behind me. I jumped up in alarm. Khadija giggled. Her husband stood there smiling. I started to rush toward my room, but she ordered me to wait. I waited. I was so dumbfounded that I'd forgotten what I was wearing, until

I caught her husband stealing glances at me. I started to back out of the room, thinking she wouldn't notice. She was speaking sharply to her husband about a personal matter between them—I don't recall what it was; I didn't even catch more than three words. But her hand shot up, signaling me to wait.

"After a bit he told her good night and turned to leave the room. On his way to the door he slowed up and gave me a complete once-over. He made no attempt to conceal it, and there was no mistaking the look in his eyes. I could feel myself shrivel. After he left, I realized she'd planned the whole thing.

"Several hours passed. I'd read three Sinbad stories to her, when suddenly she opened her eyes and asked, 'Is he back yet?'

"'Who?'

"'Yasser.' That was what he was called before our Salem came along. 'He said he had to go out and would be back later.'

"I turned to look behind me as she sniffed at the air in the direction of the open door. 'That's his cologne,' she said. 'He's back. Get me the brown attaché case from the closet.'

"I brought it over and opened it for her. She flipped through some papers, pulled out four and folded them. 'Take these to him. He's expecting them.'

"I started toward my room. 'Where're you going?' she asked.

"'To put something on.'

"'Your house robe will do.'

"I put on my robe. Only when I came back and saw the way she looked at me did I realize that the robe was almost as short as the nightgown.

"'This isn't what I picked out at the store.'

"'It looks nice on you.'

"'But it's not the one I chose.'

"'You can return it later. Or get another one.'

"I pointed down to my bare legs. She was getting impatient. 'Your legs are very pretty. Who's going to see you?'

"I bowed my head and said no more. Maybe I'm just imagining things, I thought. Maybe I was building something out of nothing. I took the papers and left the room.

"The light was on in his office. I knocked on the door. 'Come in,' he says.

"He was sitting behind his desk, talking on the phone. He signaled for me to close the door behind me. I held out the papers to him, but he ignored them and gestured me toward one of the chairs in front of his desk. I took a seat.

"When he finished his phone call, he got up and came around the desk and sat in the chair facing mine. I started to stand up, but he indicated that I should stay put. He took the papers, leafed through them quickly and muttered, 'Okay, we'll see what happens.'

"Then he said, 'And you?'

"'Me?'

"'How're things going? I know Khadija can be a bit difficult.'

"'She's not difficult at all.'

"'So you're happy?'

"'I am, God be thanked.'

"'If there's anything at all, let me know. Even if it's between you and me, I'll solve it.'

"'That's very kind of you, sir.'

"I stood up to leave. He stood up too. He reached out his hand as though to brush something off my hair. The next thing I knew it was on my cheek . . . . I did what I could. I wrenched myself free. I pushed him away. I begged and pleaded with him. I couldn't escape, no matter how hard I tried . . . . Then it was over."

She was crouched over, toward her knees, her fist pressing against her mouth. I found it hard to believe her. Many women have gone through what she did, but they never talk about it. Why her? What made her confide that to me? Her face was dark and pinched with pain, her shoulders sagging. Did telling me stories like that get her off? I sat stiffly in my chair. I had no desire to console her, or even to say a sympathetic word.

"You're probably thinking, 'Why's she telling me these things which shouldn't be told to a soul?' I'll tell you why." Her voice was faint, distant. "Every time I try to talk about myself I find myself talking about her. Now I'm going to tell you everything, every word, every action."

She paused then said, almost in a whisper, "Every day I've been telling myself that somebody else has to know what happened." She paused again, then resumed, "I stumbled out of his office. I was numb with shock. I remember picking up my robe and the other clothes he'd torn off me. I clutched them to me, afraid to drop any of them. I climbed the stairs to go to my room. I tried not to look at her before reaching my door. But she wasn't breathing heavily the way she does when she's asleep. Out of the corner of my eye, I could see her lying there, still, pretending to be asleep. She'd been awake the whole time, waiting for me to come back. I lay down in my bed, just as I was, and closed my eyes.

"Next morning, I was woken by the daylight pressing on my eyelids. She was leaning over me—she, who can barely budge two inches on her own, had made her way into my room.

She'd have had to support herself on every piece of furniture or wall she could grab a hold of. I sat up so quickly it made me dizzy. Her heavy hand pushed me back to rest. I know my nightgown was wrinkled and my hair was a mess—she was smoothing it down with her hand. I could barely bring myself to look at her. She looked so content, better than I'd seen her in a long time. She stroked my cheek then brought her hand to my mouth and placed her finger over my lips. She smiled. 'Tomorrow we'll talk. Go back to sleep.'

"'Should I help you back to your room?'

"'I'll go back the same way I came. Now, sleep.'

"As she turned around, she noticed the clothes I'd dropped on the floor next to my bed the night before. She looked back to study me for a moment, then made her way to the door, using the wall to keep herself propped up."

14

"She didn't call for me as she normally does early every morning. I overslept. When I went into her room, I found her in bed, the breakfast tray on the table. She greeted me with a huge smile and said, 'I waited for you so we could have breakfast together.'

"This was so unusual that I could only gape, unable to say a word. Then I went and took a shower, came back, and had breakfast with her. When we'd finished, she nodded toward the bed and said, 'Let's have our coffee over there.'

"I helped her lie down, placed the two bolsters behind her back and sat down in your chair to make the coffee.

"'So tell me about it,' she said.

"'About what?'

"'About what happened.'

"'You know what happened.'

"'I want to hear from you.'

"'But you already know.'

"'Tell me how he took you.'

"So I told her. She'd interrupt me with questions and I'd answer. She had to know every single detail, even the words he whispered, though I had been in such a state that I could barely remember them. She was glowing. To tell the truth, I was frightened. She was acting so strange. I told myself, 'Calm down, Zahiya. It can't get any worse than it already is.' But my fear was so strong that it blocked out that thought, blocked out everything. I asked myself, 'Where's all this going to end?'

"So I kept talking. I was too afraid to hide anything or to be embarrassed. And she kept telling me, 'Try. It'll come back to you. Just keep trying.'

"And I did try, and it did come back to me and I told her everything I remembered. Every once in a while, she'd nod and mutter, 'Yes, that's Yasser alright. He hasn't changed a bit.'

"Eventually, I asked her the question that had been nagging at me. 'Did you arrange the whole thing?'

"'I did some arranging, but not everything.'

"'And the nightgowns and underwear, you're the one who chose them?'

"'Uh-huh. I had you go to the store just so they could know your size.'

"'What else did you arrange?'

"'I just fixed it so he could see you. I had nothing to do with anything that happened after that. Look, I'm going to tell you something.' She took a couple of sips of coffee, handed me the empty cup and settled back onto her pillows. Then she started talking . . . ."

15

"She said, 'Since I've been bed bound, he started to sleep with me less and less often. Eventually he stopped coming to see me at all unless I sent a message down saying that I had to speak with him. And when he came, he was always in a rush. He had to go here, had to go there. Had work to do in the office. I always found an excuse for him. What man would want a woman in my condition? Not that I felt the urge, myself, anymore. Still, I didn't like the idea of him having an apartment in the suburbs for his affairs. Every day it's a different girl. He picks them up wherever he goes: nightclubs, hospitals, stores. They practically throw themselves at him—at him and at other men. I know Yasser. In the first years of our marriage he wouldn't even look at another woman. He was kind and he had taste. What changed him? Now he'll take anything. He probably sleeps with them once and then forgets them. I'm not sure, but those types couldn't satisfy anyone. They're not pretty or anything. I mean, what do you expect from a woman who moves from man to man? The cleaning lady at that apartment sneaks snapshots of the girls he brings there and shows them to me. When I look at those pictures, I'm amazed and I feel sorry for him. He's my husband, Zahiya. I can't stand seeing that happen to him, not to the man who I spent the best years of my life with. He could get another wife; it's his right. But he wouldn't do that to me. I'm still me, no matter what happened to my body, and he loves me. I thought about it over and over. I thought, if only I knew one girl, just one girl who I could choose to fill the gap I left in him, who would make him feel that he didn't need other women. And all this time you were with me, but I didn't see you. A whole year went by before it clicked. That was yesterday. I used to be like you before I filled out. I had the same figure as yours, your kind of beauty, your same sweet and easy-going nature. I said to myself, he'll never find another one like you and with you there he'll never need another woman. I know Yasser. He's a good man and he'll take good care of you. When I saw the way he looked at you last night, it reminded me of the way he used to look at me before we got married, and I thought, you're exactly what I'm look-ing for; I'll never find another like you. There. Now I've told you everything. Oh! One more thing: don't ever let on that I know what's going on between you. He's the one who saw you and picked you out. And don't go to him. Let him come to you. Me, I sleep early. And another thing: refuse any gift he tries to give you, no matter how much he insists. I know, I know, it's not in your nature to accept. I can't remember how many times I've offered you something and you refused. There now, that's all I have to say.'

"I couldn't believe my ears. What's happened to the world, I thought. Could a woman really go that far no matter how wretched she is? My head was spinning with words no one in their right mind would ever expect to hear. But there was no getting away; she kept me by her side the whole day long. 'Sit down,' she'd say. So I'd sit. 'Read me a Sinbad story.' So I'd read her a Sinbad story. And while I was looking at the book I could feel her eyes on my face as she said, 'Do you remember, Zahiya? I must have told you . . . about when I cried on the chest of that boy. When you asked me his name, I said I couldn't remember. His name was Zayed. I just didn't feel like telling you his name before. He held me to him while I cried, with his hand on my backside. I've never forgotten it for a moment. It's been years and years. Even after I got married I couldn't forget it. It flashes to mind—I can't say why—as though it happened yesterday. His arms around me, my face against his chest, I clutch him tightly as I cry, afraid he'll let go. There's nobody else in the world I want but him. Ah! Life.'

"My head was aching from those stories of hers about her childhood and that boy. She'd stop and start up again. On and on she'd go.

"That evening, after reading a few more pages from *A Thousand and One Nights*, she grew drowsy. 'Lay me down,' she said, so I helped her get ready for sleep. On my way to my room she said, 'Take a shower before you go to bed. And open the closet. On the third shelf where the perfumes are, you'll find a box with Firenza written on it.'

"I took out the box she'd indicated and turned to her. She was facing the other way. She said, 'Take it. I've had it for nine years. I've been saving it for the day when I get my health back. If he's still like he used to be, he'll come to your room tonight.'

"She didn't even glance in my direction. She made no movement at all, as though she hadn't said anything out of the ordinary. I stood there for a moment watching her still body while holding this bottle of perfume that I didn't want. I was afraid to put it back in the closet because she'd hear the noise and snap at me. So I set the bottle down on the dresser and headed to my room, thinking, what nonsense. He would never come up here and go through her bedroom on the way to mine.

"Before I reached my door, she asked, 'Did you take the perfume?'

"I went back to the dresser and picked up the bottle."

Dawn had begun to glow faintly on the horizon. Perhaps Zahiya noticed me looking out the window because she said, "I'm sorry. I lost all sense of time. I just kept talking and talking, and I didn't even get around to what I meant to tell you."

Her head was tilted against the headboard. Dark circles rimmed her eyes. "You'll visit again soon?"

I said that I would.

16

I t was the twilight before dawn.

The cool air braced me. I felt like taking a walk. As I replayed her story in my mind, it began to lose its freshness. I must have left bits out. While I was with her, I was inclined to believe her. Perhaps it was the way her face colored as she spoke. Afterward she said, "Bear with me and you'll know everything." What more could she possibly have to tell? She's alone there in the villa. She could roam through its dozens of rooms, sit on whatever balcony suited her mood, or stroll among the trees in the garden, clutching her robe around her. There's a rocking chair in the garden. Even if she saw it, she'd probably pass by it without thinking to try it out. Nor would it occur to her to take a dip in the swimming pool, which always lures the domestics when the masters of the house are away. Television? I doubt it; she's never mentioned it. She probably just walks, pacing the garden paths until her feet wear out. Or maybe she confines herself to the rooms and corridors of the mansion. I picture her in those vast chambers, weaving around the large plush chairs and sofas, taking care not to bump into the delicate little side tables and low coffee tables that populate the rooms. Not that she's ever spoken of her rambles through the villa. It has probably never occurred to her to mention it. Why should she? All alone in the vacant house, she goes out of one room and into the next, passes through corridors, opens some doors and takes a peek, night after night, until she finally ends up in the room she's grown used to. She sits on the armchair next to the bed. The image of Umm Salem sprawled out on the bed appears to her, as she recalls the stories her mistress related to her year in and year out. She probably sits there for hours. What else does she have to do? When does she sleep? When does she wake up?

Suddenly I realized that my feet had led me back to Abu Salem's villa. I saw her standing on her balcony, resting her elbows on the railing. I turned and stared at her. She stared back, remaining still and solemn. Out of the corner of my eye, I caught sight of some people making their way toward the nearby mosque for dawn prayers. I headed in their direction.

17

The worshipers ranged themselves in rows behind the imam. Many were yawning, having just arrived from the festivities in the stadium or elsewhere. From those I spoke with before prayers I learned that the parties that had been held in the various parts of town had been less raucous than the celebrations in the stadium. Also, they had apparently decided to go to the mosque closest to their homes so that they could get to bed as soon as possible after prayers.

The imam held us back after prayers. For a supplication, he told us as he turned to face the mihrab again, palms up. He remained silent and motionless until he could hear that we were all back in place and still.

"God grant victory to the Emirate team," he intoned.

"Amen," we chanted.

"May God crown their heads with the laurel of victory."

"Amen."

"And return them to us safely."

"Amen."

18

The Filipinos and I threw ourselves into the task of sprucing up the grounds. We pruned the trees, trimmed the hedges, mowed the lawn, washed down the outside and inside stairways, emptied out the swimming pool and scrubbed down its walls and the deck area. It took us three days. We worked from noon, when we woke up, until sunset, when we went to the stadium for the evening. The women set about spring-cleaning the inside of the villa. They brought out all the mattresses and upholstered furniture to air in the sun, calling us over from time to time to help them lift the heavier items. Whenever I left the villa during this time, I avoided passing in front of Abu Salem's place. Perhaps I feared hearing the sequel. To keep myself busy, I also helped clean and rearrange all the storerooms.

The next match was coming up soon. In the evenings in the stadium, I moved from group to group. I also enlisted with the Egyptian band. They issued me a khaki uniform and a red tarboosh, and affixed a large drum to my belly. "Rat-a-tat, boom, boom," I went as we marched in the arena to wild cheers and applause. In our breaks, my fellow band members and I drank licorice tea served to us by another of our countrymen. Harnessed to his right side was a huge glass urn filled with the brown liquid, the customary ball of red loofah dangling from the neck of the urn, while attached to his left side was the aluminum rack for carrying the glasses. In one hand, he carried the hand symbols that announced his calling, in the other a pitcher of water for rinsing out the glasses. A sprig of fresh basil was tucked behind his ear. He could have come straight from the Sayyida Zeinab or Hussein quarters in Cairo.

One evening, I joined a group of Jordanians and partook of their "kabsa." They were seated on the ground around a huge platter piled with a pyramid of rice and lamb. As I was passing, I slowed to inhale the thick waves of aromatic steam rising from the food that had been freshly ladled onto the platter. One of the diners reached up, took hold of my elbow and pulled me down into their circle as the others slid over to make place. We ate with our right hand, working the hot rice into balls in our palms and then popping them into our mouths.

In the midst of the preparations for the national team's next game in two days time, an oil pipeline burst. Foreign workers collected in front of the police stations to learn more news and offer to help in any way. I joined the men that assembled in front of the police station near Abu Amer's villa. The Indian officer in charge came out and told us that the problem was with a major pipeline that transports oil to Europe. The technicians had gone out to the site of the damage, located deep in the desert. He was still awaiting instructions.

We sat for a while outside on the grass. It was nearing sunset. Shortly after the sun had set, the Indian officer came out again and told us that anyone with a car should drive volunteer workers out to the site. We would be under the orders of the technicians there. There were couplings that had to be dismantled and repaired or replaced.

Three multi-lane tarmac highways stretch out from the capital city deep into the desert. Hundreds of cars sped along one of them in parallel lines. A small group of engineers waved us down at some distance from the site. Cranes, excavators, and powerful floodlights had preceded us. Engines were rumbling a short way off.

Seven couplings had to be extracted and replaced. An engineer came up and took twenty men over to the site, then returned to take ten more. The rest of us leaned against the hoods of the cars and waited. Although most of us—including me—were not needed, we continued to idle not far from the worksite.

The repairs were completed by sunrise. The senior engineer gave the order to turn on the pumps again. An hour later, he ordered the men to refill the ditches.

We remained by our cars until the engineers took off back to the city. We followed in a long convoy behind them. We slept most of the rest of the day.

19

I was going to go to the stadium to watch the match. The men and women at the villa had already left. We'd arranged to meet at the women's tent for the grilled quails and pigeons they had planned for dinner.

I pulled out of the driveway and got out of the car to shut the gate. I tried to resist glancing at the villa next door. Those stories of hers. They made me feel lost. I didn't know whether to believe them or not. They were spinning me through emotions I had never experienced before, and now they had taken an ominous turn. If it were just my own anguish I had to deal with, I could continue to listen, but some alarm was warning me to stop.

As I stood at the gate, I thought just one glance as I drive off. Even if she's on the balcony, she won't see me inside my car. I got in and drove off slowly. As I passed in front of Abu Salem's I spotted her leaning on the railing of the balcony. Almost instinctively, I pulled over and got out. She straightened up and, instead of her usual furtive signal, she waved me toward the gate as though indifferent to whether anyone saw her.

I passed through the gate, down the footpath and up the few steps to the front door where she was waiting. After I stepped inside, she closed the door and turned to face me. "I've been waiting for you for days. I was afraid you wouldn't come back. I blame myself. I felt I must have annoyed you in some way."

"I was very busy."

To my surprise, she had not taken her usual care with her appearance. Her hair was disheveled with strands of lint caught in it. She wore a dark, shapeless housecoat that buttoned in front and an ordinary housedress beneath. Its collar, which showed above the V of the housecoat, was trimmed with a thin ribbon of black lace.

"Busy?" There was a note of reproach in her voice as she darted her eyes at me sideways and then headed up the stairs.

We took our usual seats: me in the armchair, her on the edge of the bed with one foot drawn up beneath her. Her face had grown even paler.

"I haven't made dinner. If you like, I could . . . ."

"I'm not hungry right now. If I want anything I'll tell you."

She gave a weak smile then said, "They'll be back soon."

"Who knows? If the team wins the next two matches, they could be away much longer."

"She hasn't even called once. Just to ask how I'm doing. There was a time when she wouldn't let me out of her sight for a second, until she wanted to go to sleep. But, what would she have to say, anyway? I mean, after what happened?—Oh, Zahiya, how could you forget again?" She got up and brought over the low side table and paraphernalia for tea.

"We don't choose what we forget. All day long, I forget to do this or that, or look for something because I can't remember where I put it. I didn't used to be that way, as anyone

93

here will tell you. In fact, they'd come to me to ask after the things that they had misplaced. Only Umm Salem was better at it. She never leaves her bed unless it's to go the bathroom, but she knows where every last thing in the house is. She can tell you how many of them there are and their colors. I guess that I gradually came to depend on her memory. She doesn't miss a thing. The first time her husband came to my room—I wasn't even thinking about him; she's the one who let me know he'd be coming. Did I tell you this already? She said, 'Take your bath before you go to bed. And take that bottle of that perfume from Florence and put on the cinnamon-colored satin nightgown.'

"She was lying on her side in her sleeping position, but there wasn't a hint of drowsiness in her eyes. I went into my room thinking I'm not going to do a word she says. After a moment the bell on my bedstead buzzed insistently. I went back into her room.

"'I didn't hear you take your bath.'

"'I was just about to.'

"'Take it in there.' She indicated her bathroom—there's a shelf full of bath oils in there.

"I took my bath in there.

"Back in my room, I couldn't sleep. What if he came? I got out of bed and put on the satin nightgown she'd picked out—I was sure she'd find out if I hadn't worn it—and dabbed on a bit of the Firenza. I climbed back into bed. What ever was I thinking? It was all so weird, from beginning to end. I didn't have the faintest idea what to do. Should I get up and bolt the door? But if he came, as she said he would, he'd try the handle once and give up. He knows that the slightest noise would wake her. And what would she say or do to me if she found out I'd bolted the door? There was no getting around her.

"He came—as quiet as a mouse. I didn't even hear the door open and shut. A sliver of light slipped in from the other room and then vanished. That was all.

"He tiptoed up to the head of my bed. He reached out and touched my face. I wanted to fight him off, but I didn't.

"Afterward, he stretched out beside me and fell asleep. I stayed awake. He didn't sleep long—half an hour. He sat up and waited another half hour, then left. When did I fall asleep? I was woken by the sunlight glaring through the window. I'd forgotten to close the curtains.

"I found her sitting at the table, reading a newspaper. The table was set for breakfast and the dishes of food were still covered. I'd never seen her read a newspaper before. She greeted me with a big smile, saying, 'I thought I'd let you sleep in today. Go wash up and then we'll have breakfast together.'

"I took a shower. When I returned she indicated the chair opposite hers, so I took a seat. We ate our breakfast in silence, but all the while I could feel her stealing glances at my face.

"After I put her back in bed, I returned to my room to tidy it up. After a little while she rang for me. I knew exactly what she wanted. I waited until I composed myself and then went to her. She rolled slightly to the side so she could face me. 'So he came, like I said he would?'

"'Yes. He came.'

"'What's got into you?'

"'All your questions.'

"I don't know how I found the courage to speak to her in that tone. But she laughed and said, 'You mean, I'm asking you about things that are none of my business?'

"'I didn't say that.'

"'But you felt like saying it.' When I didn't reply she said, 'Go make some coffee and then come back here so I can talk to you.' I did as instructed.

"While we were having coffee she said, 'Zahiya, you're part of me now. What goes for me goes for you. What I'd like to do, you can do. So when I ask you about him it's to make sure you're alright, because if you're alright, I'm alright. I can see from the look on your face that you're beginning to take a liking to him. In two or three days he'll come here and tell us that he's locked up the apartment in the suburbs, or sold it. He'll be the old Yasser, again. The Yasser I've always known. So tell me, what did he say to you last night?'

"Her question took me by surprise. I hesitated at first, but the way she beamed at me reassured me a bit. I related every word I could remember. Now and then she'd nod and say, 'Yes, that's what he used to say to me. I was afraid those other women might have changed him. But he's still the same. Did he fall asleep right afterward?'

"'A little bit afterward.'

"'Facing you?'

"'Yes.'

"'With his arm on top of you?'

"'Uh-huh.'

"'That's Yasser alright. And when he left?'

"'When he left?'

"'Yes. Did he lean over and whisper to you?'

"'He leaned over and kissed me.'

"He didn't kiss me. I'd invented that. By that point I couldn't help myself. I had to hurt her. At first I thought I'd succeeded. She stared at me intently with a glimmer of doubt

96

in her eyes. Then she smiled and said, 'No he didn't. Anyway, what counts is that what we wanted to happen happened.'

"It was what *she* had wanted to happen. All I wanted was to get out of the situation without causing more problems for myself.

"She contemplated me for a moment then said, 'I was going to tell you something. But after what I heard and saw it's not necessary.'

"'What were you going to say?'

"'That you're fond of him. As long as you want him, you'll do it on your own. Every woman does as she sees fit.'

"She was toying with me like a cat with something in its clutches. I could feel myself losing my temper. 'What am I going to do on my own?'

"She gave me a patient smile. 'You see? You've already become touchy. Listen, I'm not trying to hurt you. I'd never think of it. I just wanted to warn you about something in his character.'

"I collected myself and held my tongue. She said, 'Don't play hard to get. Some women think that by doing that they can make a man more attached to them. Sometimes they overdo it. With Yasser it doesn't work at all. I tried it once. He left the room and didn't sleep with me again for about a month. When he saw how hard I was trying to make amends he softened and returned to normal.'"

Zahiya fell silent. She rubbed her palms back and forth on the fabric of her housecoat at her knees. She seemed about to continue. But she must have caught me glancing at my watch, because she said in a weary voice, "It's about time for the soccer match, I think."

"It is."

"I'm a bit tired anyway. I don't know what's happened to me. The smallest effort seems to wear me out."

I had stood up by then. She stayed on the bed with her head bowed.

20

The excitement at the stadium picked my spirits up. The bleachers were packed. Women were in the aisles and the spaces between the rows tending to pots of food. On the field, a succession of dancing and singing troupes took turns performing their acts while a team of runners jogged around the circumference parading a long multicolored streamer over their heads in a way that made it wave and shimmer beneath the glare of the floodlights. The video displays mounted on the upper rims of the stadium were broadcasting the introductory coverage. I still had time to get a bite to eat before the match began.

I paused uncertainly when I noticed a gathering of Pakistani women in the clearing in front of the tents. The maids from Abu Amer's villa were in front. One of them pointed toward me, rose up on her knees and waved to me with both arms. I spotted Rishim among the women laying out trays of food in the center of a large circle of men. The three Filipinos seemed out of place in that Pakistani gathering. They cleared a space for me and before I knew it, I had a plate piled with grilled pigeon and quail before me. I turned my attention to Rishim.

She hadn't even noticed me. Following the direction of her gaze I spotted her husband sitting among the other men. The two were exchanging wordless messages with their eyes. A secret smile played on her lips as she offered pieces of quail to the men, or ladled out rice mixed with nuts and raisins. As she held out the bottle of hot sauce to her husband, another man's arm reached out to grab it, but her eyes remained fixed on her husband's. They must have reached some understanding: they'd continue to keep their marriage hidden and only meet in the presence of others. It was too dangerous to advertise their secret.

The game ended in the defeat of the Emirati team. The stadium was plunged into a dismal silence. Eyes remained riveted on the screens in disbelief until they were turned off. Then the floodlights were extinguished, leaving only ordinary lamps to cast a dim glow on the playing field. Outside, scattered fires flickered among the tents. Some began to grumble at the glare from these fires in the black night and one-by-one they, too, were extinguished.

All activity inside and outside the stadium had come to a stop. Only the occasional murmur broke the silence. It was still too early to go to sleep. Even so, people stretched out on their makeshift beds and remained still until they dozed off.

21

The hope was that the team would win its next match and qualify for the next round. I watched the game in the stadium with the same rapt attention as everyone else. There was no fanfare or jubilation this time; we watched in total silence. Even the food was insipid: cheese, jam, and boiled egg sandwiches; bottled water.

The game ended in a tie. Everyone left to sleep in their own homes. No one was in the mood for entertainment or merrymaking. There was one last chance. If the Moroccan team lost in its upcoming match with Portugal, the Emirate team would still have a shot at the finals.

All conversation over the next two days revolved around how well the Moroccan team performed and its record of wins and losses. Most agreed that the odds were against it, particularly since its star player would not be playing due to a knee injury.

After the evening prayer had ended on the night before the Morocco–Portugal match we remained in our ranks behind the imam. Some of the men asked the imam to lead us in a supplication.

He snapped his head around. "A supplication for who?" He was a bald, stern looking Pakistani.

"For the defeat of the Moroccan team," one of us volunteered.

The imam frowned and said, "It's not right to invoke harm."

"There's no harm in that. It's just losing a game."

"That's not something to pray to God for."

"Then let's ask Him to help the Emirate team reach the finals."

"What kind of supplication is that? It's like asking the good Lord to help someone catch a bus."

"What if we pray for the Portuguese team to win?"

"God forbid! That's a non-Muslim nation and you want to pray for it?"

"There are Muslims there."

"Only a few. And don't forget that it was a colonial power that brought misery and degradation to the people of Africa."

"What's Africa got to do with us?"

The men had gathered around the imam, blocking his way to the door. "Please think of a way. We want to offer a supplication to God," one of them pleaded.

The imam bowed his head in thought. Then he said, "Let's go outside. There we can say whatever prayer we want."

An Indian challenged him. "The God we pray to inside the mosque is the same God we're going to pray to outside the mosque."

The Pakistani glared at him angrily. "Foolish Indian! This is a holy place."

The Indian shot back, "This is the last time I'm going to pray behind an idiot imam like you!"

In the end we went out into the street and arranged ourselves in three rows behind the imam. Before he began, he looked behind him as though about to instruct us to straighten our lines, as he always does before prayers in the mosque. However, he checked himself, faced forward, and held up his hands in supplication.

"May God defeat the Moroccan team," he intoned.

"Amen," we chorused.

"May God inflict an ignominious defeat on the Moroccan team."

"Amen."

"And blind them to the goal."

"Amen."

22

No one went to the stadium on the day of the match. People watched it from their homes, in coffeehouses, or at their workplaces. Many brought television sets to work for the purpose.

As the inmates had come to prefer to loll in the sun in the police station yards instead of wandering about town, the officers invited them to watch the game with them. The inmates hauled out the television sets to the fenced-in front lawn. The officer in charge had the honor of a chair while the rest took up places on reed mats that were unfurled on the ground. There were tea boys, but no one had the time or inclination to drink anything. Early on in the game the Moroccan team scored enough goals to win. No one was inclined to watch the second half. The inmates rolled up the mats, stored them behind the police station and took the opportunity to enjoy the last moments of sunlight.

Once again the Emirate was engulfed in silence. Everyone went home, the coffeehouses and stores locked their doors, and the streets emptied. The sportscaster appeared on television with the following announcement: "The Emirate team has been eliminated from the World Cup finals. But they left the field with their heads raised high, having executed their duty to perfection. They performed much better than the winning teams, to which the majority of sports commentators testify. Unfortunately, luck was not on our side, a factor that is ever-present in soccer and to which not even the greatest teams in the world are immune. We cannot but add that this was the first time a team from the East qualified for the World Cup finals, which, in itself, is a magnificent victory."

Soon afterward, the streetlights flickered on, the stores and coffeehouses reopened for business, people reemerged from their houses to spend the evening as usual, and life soon resumed its familiar din. Later that evening a spokesman for the municipality came on the air to announce that the following day would be "Cleaning Day." Domestics were to clean the outside walls of the houses and villas until they gleamed, wash down the trees and bushes in the gardens and along the outside pavements, and collect all litter into plastic bags which were to be deposited on the curbs for removal.

The following morning, the Filipinos and I hosed down the villa walls and the trees and the hedges in the garden, after which two of them hauled out a couple of hoses to wash down the greenery around the outside walls. The other Filipino helped to dangle me down from the roof in a loop of rope so that I could polish the outside panes and frames of the upper-story windows. I wielded a spray bottle filled with glass cleaner for the purpose. Outside the villa walls, I could hear the brushes, sprays, and humming motors of the street cleaning vehicles.

In the late afternoon, we had lunch together on the garden lawn, gazing at the results of our handiwork on the villa, which beamed in the rays of a sun heading toward the horizon.

Rishim seemed happy and content. Her eyes sparkled. I said the one expression she knows in Arabic: "Kullu tamam?"—Is everything okay?

She smiled shyly and pulled her head covering over half her face to hide her embarrassment. "Kullu tamam," she said.

One of the other women announced that they were going out together that night to buy gifts for their families. It would be a very long time before they had another such opportunity to go on a shopping excursion together.

"If you want, I can drive you to wherever you're going and come back later and pick you up," one of the Filipinos offered.

"Okay. Could you take us to the market district and pick us up in three hours?"

"Sure."

Another Filipino nodded toward the villa and asked, "Are they coming home tomorrow?"

"The team's arriving tomorrow and some of the Emiratis. The rest will be coming back on different flights," I said.

"What about Abu Amer?"

"I don't know what flight he'll be on. Maybe in a couple of days. It'll take four or five days for all of them to come back."

The Pakistani women stood up and began to clear the table. Rishim collected a few dishes and hurried into the villa ahead of the others, who watched her go inside with knowing smiles on their faces. She's probably arranged to see her husband in the market, I thought. Maybe they'll have a chance to talk and hold hands without being noticed.

After the women left, one of my coworkers sprawled out on the grass. Then he rolled to his side and propped his head up on his elbow so he could look at the rest of us. "Where to, tonight?" he asked.

"Where to? To the coffeehouse, of course. You have a better idea?" answered another.

"I do. I'm a storehouse of ideas."

"Then tell us."

"There's a Jordanian in the suburbs—I don't know which suburb; we can ask and find out. He had a premonition. Yesterday he received a sign that it would come true. He's having a big party and invited everyone who wants to come. I heard that he's arranged with some Indian friends of his to put on a singing and dancing performance. A lot of people are going."

"What was his premonition?"

"That his wife is going to die."

We burst out laughing. He rolled on the grass and howled, then sat up again. "It's the truth. I'm not joking."

"Why does he want her to die?"

"Who knows?" He pointed to me. "Ask him. He's one of them and knows them better than we do. Their men have four wives, not just one. Who knows how they find the time or the mood to fuck them all."

"And who says that they fuck them?"

They roared with laughter again. I left with a smile on my face.

23

I walked in front of Abu Salem's villa, then around the perimeter. The balconies were empty and the lights on the upper story were off. The staff must be on the ground floor, where the windows were lit. I could not help feeling guilty. I should have dropped in days ago because I knew she had more to recount. I was inclined to believe her after the state I had seen her in during my last visit. No woman would confide such things in a man she barely knew unless she was at her wits' end. Of course, I'd be powerless to help her if she were in trouble, but at least I could listen.

I stepped back into the shadows of the trees in front of the villa. She would never dare to see me while the rest of the staff was there, but there was a good chance that they would spend the evening out, shopping or visiting, like the others in Abu Amer's villa. Everyone knew that this would be their last opportunity to go out on the town together and shared the urge to take advantage of it. I imagined that pretty much all the villas would empty out that night. So I waited.

A car full of people drew out of the villa gate. Soon afterward Zahiya appeared on her balcony. Keeping my eyes on her, I moved toward the gate. She spotted me, turned and went inside.

She was waiting for me, as usual, at the front door. She led me to the stairs and we went up to the room. The low table with the tea paraphernalia had already been placed in front of the armchair. I sat down. She stood silently for a moment with her hands folded in front of her. Then she said with a faint hoarseness in her voice, "I knew you'd come. They're coming back tomorrow."

She took up her position on the bed. Her face was gaunt and pale. I was on the verge of asking her whether she was ill, but I checked myself. I did not want to risk offending her. She was wearing a short-sleeved jallabiya and a light shawl around her shoulders. Her arms were soft and delicately rounded.

"They used to be much prettier," she said languidly. "Nothing remains the same."

She asked for a cigarette and leaned over to let me light it for her.

"In six years, I've only smoked five."

"Where do you smoke them?"

"In the foyer downstairs. I find a pack of cigarettes some-body left behind, smoke one, cough my heart out, rinse my mouth out, and go back up to her. When I find myself leaning too close to her, I jerk back for fear she'll smell the smoke. She misses nothing. She knows every little thing that goes on in this villa. She also hears a lot of news about the other vil-las and relates it to me. The servants in the Emirate are like a telephone network."

She laughed. "Oh. Laughing hurts. My throat's so dry. They meet in the shops and markets and exchange news and information, and she gets it out of them. When one of her maids comes back from shopping, she calls her up here, sits her in that chair and listens while the maid tells her what she heard. The maids here like her. I too used to like her in my first year here."

She put out her cigarette halfway through.

"Oh! Who could ever have imagined? I wasn't sure I wanted to come here at first. I had a job in Egypt. I was 'Miss Zahiya' at a foreign nursery school. We looked after children up to the age of four. I had a decent salary. Anyway, to make a long story short, here I am. My title in my contract is 'companion.' When I signed it, they explained to me her condition and what would be required of me. So in the few months before I left Egypt I read. Goha stories, *A Thousand and One Nights*, tales of the caliphs and of the harems in the palaces. My husband would scour the used book stalls and bring home the types of books I was looking for. And I watched dozens of old Egyptian films, starring Stefan Rushdi and Sirag Mounir and the like, and I tried to pick up the way they moved. Oh, and I got hold of those celebrity magazines in order to bone up on all the gossip about the stars. In short, I accumulated a huge storehouse of stories to keep her entertained. Then from day one, I realized that she'd brought me here so that *she* could talk. And did she ever talk! About everything that happened to her ever since her childhood. Over and over again, about her two childhood boyfriends. She'd talk and I'd listen. That was my job, to listen. But now, after what happened, I'm not sure what my job is anymore. Even after Yasser started to come up to my room regularly she would still go on and on. He'd come to me once or twice a week. She stopped questioning me about what he did and said. She'd just give me a long appraising stare when I came out of my room the following morning and I'd find that she's already had her breakfast—one of the Pakistani maids had helped her to the table—and that my breakfast was waiting for me. After finishing breakfast, I'd make us coffee and take my seat in the armchair. She'd smile and say, 'I miss you when you sleep in. Read the newspaper first.'

"There came a day, about a month after he started coming to my room, when she said, 'He sold the apartment in the suburbs, just as I said he would. Ah, Yasser. Nobody knows him like I do.' She was jubilant. She told me that he'd taken to living in the villa again and that he was having the ground floor done up. Then she warned me never to go to his room, no matter how hard he tried to persuade me. 'Make up any excuse. Just don't go down there,' she said.

"'What kind of excuse can I give if he insists?'

"'I know you want to see him in a room that isn't your own. But if you do, you'll go down in his esteem. You'll become like all those other women. I don't want to lose you. You know I can't do without you. You're a part of me now. You'll find an excuse. Tell him that I often ring for your help during the night.'

"Just as she said, Yasser asked me to spend the night in his room. He told me he likes to wake up and find me beside him. I gave the excuse that she told me. He looked a bit dejected—I have to admit that I had begun to grow fond of him—and said, 'Yes, of course. I forgot.'

"So we continued as normal. Oh! I almost forgot. I was sitting reading the newspaper to her one day—she likes to listen to the society and crime pages—when I noticed her staring at my knee. I was wearing a short nightgown. I have a mole about the size of a chickpea just above my kneecap. She said, 'I've got one just like it, above my bellybutton. Go on.'

"I started reading again as she settled into her pillows and closed her eyes. I read one crime story, then another. When I was into the third, she said, 'Zayed. His name's Zayed.'

"She shifted in her bed so she could see me. 'Remember the boy I told you about? The one whose chest I cried on? His name's Zayed. This is the first time I've ever told anyone his name.' She lay back against the pillows. In fact, she had told me his name before. I set the newspaper down on my knees and waited for her to speak.

"'He told me once that he saw me in a dream. We were sitting in the shade of a tree behind my house. He was lying on his back with his head on my lap. When he lay like that he liked to cross one leg over the other and wave his foot. We were both so happy. He said that he had taken off all my clothes and was trying to sleep with me. He kept trying but I kept fighting him off; I wouldn't let him have me. "You saw me naked?" I said. "Uh-huh. You have a mole on your belly." I was furious. I shoved his head off my lap. He sat up in alarm. He forgot to pull his jallabiya down over his legs. They're so skinny. I yelled at him, "How dare you look at me naked!" "It was just a dream," he said. I calmed down and smoothed my hair. "How many times have you seen me?" "I'm not going to tell you." And he never did.'

"She laughed and shook her head. 'What do you think, Zahiya? Is it possible? I mean for someone to see you in a dream and see a part of you he never saw before?'

"'Uh-huh, and even more: you can dream about somebody you've never seen before in your life and then meet him in the flesh, exactly like he was in the dream.'

"'Now I understand. My breasts were small then.... I mean they were okay for my age. Whenever we met, I'd tug

112

my jallabiya to make it tighter, push my shoulders back, and thrust my chest forward. He'd notice this and say nothing—until one time he burst out, "Alright! I've seen them. I've seen them many times." At the time I mistook his meaning and felt ashamed.'

"Oh! What stories she told! What was I saying? I just follow my tongue wherever it leads. Oh yes. For five or maybe six months my situation remained as I've described it. I'd given up caring and even thinking about it. But there came a day—I'll never forget it. He was drowsing beside me. For three weeks I'd been hesitating to tell him. But then I did, 'Yasser, I'm afraid I might be pregnant.'

"He sprang to sitting so fast he startled me. He looked me straight in the eyes and said, 'What about the pill? Don't you use it?'

"'I haven't been. I never thought I'd be sleeping with any-one, so I'd stopped. Then I just forgot.'

"'Oh dear, if I'd known I'd have used a condom.' He paused for a moment, then said, 'Alright. Don't worry. Two months or more?'

"'I haven't had my period for two months.'

"'Don't worry, we'll find a solution.'

"Two days later he came. He took off his sandals as he came into my room, but stayed in his thawb. He came over and sat down cross-legged on the bed.

"After a short silence he said, 'Zahiya, I don't know what to tell you. As you know, I have no children. Khadija's never been pregnant and probably never will be. So I just put the idea out of my head. I resigned myself to my fate. It's God's will, I told myself. Then, two days ago you broke the news. I've hardly had a wink of sleep since. I'm thrilled. Don't you realize? I could finally have a son. After all I've been through, after I'd completely given up hope, I've suddenly been given this blessing. And now I'm supposed to help get rid of it? No, it's too hard. It's just too hard. I'd die. Give me any other solution, and I'll do whatever you say. Anything at all.'

"I was so stunned and scared I couldn't say a word. I started to tremble.

"'Are you crying?' he said. 'What did I say to make you cry?'

"I broke into a wail. He held me and pressed my face to his chest and murmured, 'I asked you if there were another solution. But if that's what you want, just give me a couple of days and I'll have it arranged.'

"I would never have imagined he could be so dejected. His whole body was slumped and he had this mournful look in his eyes. He said, 'There's no way out of this. I can't even marry you. It's like a divine punishment. But if that's His will, so be it.' Then he left.

"I knew I had to tell Khadija. She was relaxed when I came in. But after I started speaking she shifted in bed and glowered at me. The color had drained from her face. I was so frightened my voice stopped working.

"'Go on,' she said sharply. 'Tell it right up to the end.'

"So I did. And when I finished, she didn't budge. She just stared at the feet of the armchair.

"Then she said in a low voice, 'Take me to the bathroom.'

"I helped her to the bathroom and then helped her back into bed. She turned her face away from me and said, 'Leave me.'

"I went to my room. The next day, we had breakfast in silence. Lunch too. She'd finish her meal and I'd put her back to bed. She wouldn't ask me to stay, so I'd go back to my room.

"I had no idea what to expect. All I could do was wait.

"Two days. I'd never experienced anything like them before. No sleep. No waking up. No sitting and listening. Crying would have helped, but my tears had dried up. I just waited.

"The buzzer went off after sunset. When I went to her she said, 'Go downstairs and sit in the living room. Yasser's coming.'

"I hoped she would say more, but she didn't. Not a word.

"I went downstairs. Moments later I caught sight of him going upstairs. After a long time, I saw him leave again. I raced up to her room.

"She signaled for me to sit in the armchair. After I did, she said, 'I've spoken with Yasser. He's miserable. It just never occurred to me. Probably because I stopped thinking about having children so long ago. Anyway, what we have to do now is to come up with a solution. You want to get rid of it. Bringing it into the world would spell your death. He wants to keep it. He's wanted a child ever since we got married. We did everything we could. We went to Europe and the States. Whenever there was a glimmer of hope, it was like he came alive again. Oh! We tried for years and years. Eventually I couldn't bear his pain anymore. I told him, "Take another wife, Yasser. I'll be upset for a while, but that's not what matters." And he said, "I'll never find another woman like you, Khadija." Oh, it's so hard. Now that he has a chance of having a child, he could never bear to lose it. He'd die. I told him I'd have a word with you. We'll say it's not yours.'

"When she saw my confusion, she said, 'After you give birth we say another woman had the baby.'

"'What other woman would agree to that?'

"'Me, for instance. I'm the most obvious one. The child would take his father's name. Any other woman wouldn't

115

belong here. Who knows what would happen? She'd probably want to marry Yasser, and neither you nor I would like that. And how would she treat the child? I've been thinking about this all day. If you agree, we'll arrange everything.'

"We spoke for a while more, and finally I agreed. Her solution seemed reasonable. It would keep both me and the child safe.

"That same day they announced that she was pregnant.

"'Nobody will believe it,' I told her.

"'Why shouldn't they believe it? Modern medicine works miracles. And I won't have any visitors or let anyone in this room but you.'

"And that's exactly what happened. She and I stayed pent up in here like prisoners. Nobody was allowed in, not even the servants. One of the Pakistani maids would leave our meals on a tray outside the bedroom door and return later to pick up the tray with our empty dishes on it and the laundry basket.

"Yasser received well-wishers—relatives, friends, and acquaintances—downstairs. Apparently no one thought it out of the ordinary that Khadija was pregnant. Many women get pregnant after years of despair.

"When they asked to see her, he'd apologize. 'Doctor's orders,' he told them. 'It's her condition, you know.'

"Yasser would come up to visit us practically every night. He didn't come to me in my room anymore. He'd sit with the two of us for a while, ask how we were doing and leave. When our eyes met, he'd smile—a faint smile. I wasn't sure what he meant by it. Maybe it was to reassure me.

"Khadija looked after me. She, herself, made me my glass of warm milk every morning. She'd pick out the types of food that were good for my condition and put them on my plate.

Every morning she took my temperature. She took care not to upset me and tried to make me laugh.

"She asked me, 'Which would you rather have, a boy or a girl?'

"'If I could choose, it would be a boy. I already have a girl.'

"'Me, I'd choose a girl. Yasser would want a boy, I'm sure.'

"'What do you think? Should we decide on a name now? You first.'

"She made a list of the names we agreed on and said, 'I'll show it to Yasser so he can choose too.'

"A British doctor came regularly to check my progress. Khadija fired questions at her in English then turned to me to tell me I was doing fine.

"We played cards, we watched television, pieced together jigsaw puzzles that Yasser brought, and she talked and told me stories, and the day would pass.

"My last month of pregnancy was very difficult. I'd wake up after passing out and find her next to me drying the sweat off my face with a moist cloth—the doctor said no air conditioning—and she'd lift my head in order to put a glass to my lips. I don't know what I drank. I never asked.

"I gave birth in my bedroom. Khadija stationed herself on a chair in front of my bedroom door, which stayed locked. The British doctor delivered the child. It was a boy.

"After Salem was born, the ground floor was nonstop commotion, from morning to night. Khadija said it was all the people coming to offer congratulations. She was with me most of the time, giving orders to the nurse who remained with me for a week after delivery.

"The birth certificate was drawn up as agreed: the father, Yasser; the mother, Khadija. Even so, those words on the certificate pained me.

117

"Salem stayed with me for a week. I breastfed him and the nurse cleaned him, changed his diapers, and laid him back on the bed next to me.

"Then visitors were allowed up. She lay in bed, covered with a light sheet with Salem next to her in his blanket. Chairs had been placed a short distance away from the bed for the women to sit in. I stood at the door to my bedroom. Although I had a small chair beside me, I preferred to stand so I could see Salem. Every once in a while, the women would get up and lean over the bed to watch Salem yawn or suck his fingers. They would laugh and say things like, 'He looks just like you,' and 'Spitting image.'

"And she'd smile and say, 'He takes after Yasser more.'

"She'd go on to describe what a difficult pregnancy she had, all the aches and pains she felt, how his kicking would wake her up and she'd have to shout at him, 'Be quiet, now. I want to sleep,' and how he'd immediately stop kicking.

"Those were the aches and pains I'd complained about during my pregnancy. Even that bit about Salem kicking inside the womb I'd told her about. She related all these experiences as though they were hers. She didn't make a word up. I was amazed at how completely she'd taken in everything I'd told her. And the sincerity in her voice was incredible. I don't know why this disturbed me so much.

"They redecorated a room downstairs for Salem. It's very pretty and well ventilated. They hung a lot of different colored toys over his crib. They made gentle rattling sounds. The British nanny slept in there too. That upset me. I would have preferred him to be with me, but I kept my mouth shut. The nanny was very neat and clean, and she had a kind, smiling face, which reassured me a bit.

"I'd go in there at nursing times, barely able to hold back my tears as I fed him. The nanny observed me with curiosity and cautioned me, with gestures, not to feed him when I was so worked up.

"She took him up to Khadija twice a day. I'd be there waiting. Khadija would take him in her arms, rock him gently, and murmur to him and he'd gurgle back. She'd tickle his chin with her finger, lay him on the pillow next to her and whisper to him, too softly for me to hear. When he grew some and his babbling got louder and he began to move his limbs more, she'd bare his legs and let him play with them next to her in the patch of sunlight on her bed.

"I adjusted. There was no other way. I could see Salem whenever I wanted and stay in his room and play with him. Maybe they told everyone else that I was his nanny or his wet nurse; I never asked. Only at his nap times was I forbidden to go into his room. One day the British nanny barred the way. It only happened once. I never tried again. She stood on the other side of the door, holding it slightly ajar, pointed to Salem and pressed her hands to her cheek to mime sleep. I stood there wavering for a moment then went back upstairs. It would have been better if he slept in my arms, with me patting him on the back and stroking his hair until he dozed off. It's not as though I haven't raised children before.

"On my way back and forth to his room, I'd have to pass by Yasser's office. Sometimes he'd be standing at the door. I'd slow up a bit and we'd exchange smiles. He wouldn't ask me inside. Not that I wanted to go in there. I no longer felt the same toward him. I don't know what happened. He's as kind and considerate as always. It's just that things returned to the way they were before he first visited my room.

"Khadija's the one who has me confused. It's not that we had an argument or that she hurt me in any way. But she doesn't need me any more. We don't have breakfast together, or our morning coffee. We barely talk any more. It's as though she's washed her hands of me. I come into her room in the morning and find that she's already had her breakfast and drank her coffee. My breakfast is waiting for me on the table. I eat it, sit in the armchair and wait. She's absorbed in a serial on the radio. She laughs and says, 'What a sense of humor!'

"She goes from one serial to the next; then watches television or the video—she has a huge video collection—until eventually I give up waiting for her to speak and go back into my room. She doesn't even have me help her into the bathroom in the middle of the night. She rings for one of the Pakistani maids instead.

"I've begun to ask myself what I'm doing here. I receive my salary like clockwork at the first of every month. I find it in an envelope on my nightstand. I don't know what to do with the money. I haven't done any work to earn it. I used to give it to the driver to wire it to my account in Egypt. Often Yasser would see me handing the envelope to the driver and say, 'The bank's on my way. Give it to me and I'll transfer it for you.' Now I just slip it into the drawer on top of the last envelope.

"Salem's grown a lot. He plays in the garden with the nanny. I stand a little way off and watch. I can't bear his indifference to me and his absorption in his games as though I'm not there. I've tried every trick in the book to draw his attention and get him to come to me. He just stares at me in wonder and then looks around for his nanny.

"I see him when he comes up to Khadija's room. He throws himself into her open arms and snuggles into her fleshy chest.

They whisper to each other, too softly for me to make out what they're saying from where I'm standing. She acts as though I'm not there. I shift uncomfortably, feeling that I'm intruding and, at the same time, hoping that she'll see me and call me over to talk with him.

"He's so far away and growing further away the older he gets. I watch him from a distance, because I've begun to sense his discomfort when I'm too close. Once, when he was playing in the garden, I moved to within a couple of steps from him. He whispered something to the nanny who turned to me with a frown. I'm supposed to be a companion. That's what I was hired for. Now I don't know what my job is."

I'd been leaning forward staring at the carpet in order to avoid looking at her. I'd expected a sob when she'd finished. To my surprise, when I sat up I found that, although her hands were clenched in her lap, her eyes were dry and her pallid face was calm.

After a long silence she said, "I wonder what you think about me now."

I gave her a sympathetic smile.

"I felt like telling you about myself and now I have. I don't think we're going to see each other again."

I stood up, unable to find the right words. We exchanged a last glance and I left. I went straight back to my room at Abu Amer's, telling myself, "I am not going to think about a thing."

24

The streets were decked with victory arches made of flowers. Each was crowned with a photo of one of the members of the national soccer team, intercepting the ball with the edge of his foot.

I passed by the police station on my way to the parade. The Indian officer in charge was in his official uniform: dark green with yellow stripes on the epaulets. He was just inside the door, standing at attention, his twirled mustache glistening with grease and his gun hanging in its holster at his side. The prisoners were back behind bars. Their arms reached through the windows waving miniature national flags. Women and children had collected at the windows and on the balconies overlooking the street.

I stood with the throngs that packed the sides of the road leading from the airport to the capital. We were waiting to cheer the returning team. Songs in various languages were blaring from the tape recorders some of the spectators had brought with them. Here and there the crowds made way for circles of jubilant celebrators who sang and danced. I could hear the Egyptian ditty: "Safe and sound, safe and sound. We left and came back safe and sound."

The team drove slowly by in open vehicles, waving beneath the raining petals. After the procession passed, the crowds ran after it.

I waited until the noise subsided and the road cleared. Then I returned to the villa.

Acknowledgments

The translator would like to express his gratitude to Dr. Hala Halim, who helped make this book possible.

Modern Arabic Literature

The American University in Cairo Press is the world's leading publisher of Arabic literature in translation.

For a full list of available titles, please go to:

mal.aucpress.com